Seven Sordid Stories

Nick Swain

NEW PULP PRESS

Published by New Pulp Press, LLC, 926 Truman Avenue, Key West, Florida 33040, USA.

For information contact:
Publisher@NewPulpPress.com

ISBN-13: 978-1945734236 (New Pulp Press)

ISBN-10: 194573423X

Printed in the United States of America
Visit us on the web at www.newpulppress.com

1

Blood on the Curb
Part One

Little Man, Small World

I

The dice bounced off the wall and rattled against the sidewalk. A single pip in each bone-hued cube peered back up at the boys huddled around them; all baby-faced, all in caps and knickers. "Snake Eyes!" the young roller shouted triumphantly. "My go again."

"That ain't how you play!" exclaimed the blonde boy opposite him, the black of his pupils widening, besieged by frustration.

"That's how we play. And you either get with it or scram!"

"Fine." The blonde boy submitted. "But make it double or nothing!" He took a velvet-foiled bar from his back pocket and snapped it in two, dropping one half into the pot on the pavement, composed mostly of broken chocolates, taffy, and chewing gum. The first young boy scooped the dice up and shook them by his ear. "Come on, eleven ... papa needs eleven, baby..."

In front of the building where the boys were shooting dice, a sky-blue Cadillac coupe pulled to the curb. As its driver finished parking, the passenger emerged; a towering, swart man dressed in a smart blue suit, starting straight toward the boys. The blonde one had begun to scuffle with the other as he attempted to pocket his winnings. "You chiseling weasel, you snatched 'em up before I could even see!" the blonde boy insisted.

1

The darker haired boy began to get the better of him, as the others egged them on – not cheering for anyone in particular. The tall man stepped in, tugging them each up and apart by their shirts. "What the hell's the matter with you brats?"

"He's a dirty cheat!" the blonde started again, unfazed.

"Am not!" the other shouted, the man's powerful arms the only thing keeping them apart.

"Cut it out," the man spoke curtly. "I'm talkin' 'bout the dice. You kids stupid or somethin'? Shootin' craps out here on the sidewalk, in front of God an all these businesses, not even using the perfectly good alley you got right beside you? You rugrats are ridin' the fast rails to the reformatory with gags like that!"

"We weren't betting nothing but chocolates, mister," one boy spoke up.

The man scoffed. "You think any of the coppers out here'll care that you're just playin' for candies? All they'll see is a gang of hoods in the making, and then *BAM*, that's exactly what you'll be before you can even decide for yourself.

"Alright, go on. Beat it. And if you ain't goin' to school like you should then find a rooftop or an alley to do that in – and not *this alley!*"

The gang of boys broke into a lope, scurrying down the sidewalk as the second man emerged from the car. "Nothing changes, huh?" he said. His skin too was naturally dark, and he had the same oval-shaped face and high-cheekbones his passenger did.

"No, nothin' changes." The men stood in front of the store, admiring the inside through a wide-pane window. Inside there was row after row of liquor bottles; in the window, on the high-selves lining all four walls, even behind the counter. To the west of the shop, from under a hanging sign that read *Sallie's Shoe Shop*, a man with thick, iron-gray hair and mustache was sweeping the doorway. He stopped to wave at the boys and greet them, his heavy Neapolitan accent present in each syllable. The two men greeted him in return. "Hey how's it goin' Mr. Terizini?" An older woman passed the shop pushing a baby carriage. A few stores down, the young boys had started a new game despite still being within sight of their banisher. The first man smirked and started to the store, noticing the other was not following. "What's the matter? You got the key, don't you?"

"Yea. I was just thinking."

"'Bout what, that dish comin' up the sidewalk? I don't blame you."

"No."

The first man eyed the other over solemnly. "You worried?"

The man shrugged. "Got to be, with their kind."

"Well nothin' will change inside. Come on."

The men started toward the stores entrance, the first dragging behind to watch the approaching woman he'd mentioned. From the other side of his shoulder came a voice. "Anthony?"

The man's right hand quickly – almost instinctively, found its way inside his jacket; the left holding the flap open at a discreet angle, not quite revealing what he might've been holding. But when he saw the diminutive owner of that shrill voice he came out empty-handed, all smiles. "Anthony Giante?" A wiry little man, with naturally nervous eyes set in a round face under the lowered brim of a hat, stood between him and the Cadillac.

"Mannie? I can't freakin' believe it, Mannie?" The man looked over to his companion at the door. "Look Sam! It's Mannie, from Stateville!"

3

The second man gestured dutifully from the door, standing by, unamused and waiting. Not as pleased with his surprise guest.

"Jesus, Mannie! So how the hell you been? *Sam!* Sam, get over here, it's Mannie!"

But he was already turning the key and opening the door. "Yea, be there in a minute. Gotta open up first, we've got a business to run again, you know."

Anthony clucked his tongue distastefully as Sam disappeared into the store, then patted the short man on the arm. "See the outside hasn't made you any taller, huh Man?"

"Yea. Yea," the short man answered absently, his dark eyes moving rapidly over the store. "What ... What're you doing these days?"

"Oh, admirin' the scenery." Anthony smiled as a strawberry blonde in a mink coat strutted by, hardly paying any mind. From the East, the blonde boy was working back down the sidewalk, inspecting each crevice and crack in the concrete. He seemed to have lost something. "How's the real world been treatin' you?"

"Where's Sam?" The short man blurted, still not making eye-contact with Anthony. "Sam should be here too!"

Anthony frowned. "What'd you go deaf the last few months? Didn't you hear him? He said he'd be back in a second."

But the small man didn't seem to hear that either. He was looking into the street now.

"I see you're still a jitter-bug, Mannie. Why don't you hang back and take in the sights?" Two more young, attractive women came walking by from the West; one with red-hair under a smart hat, the other a blonde. Anthony tipped his hat to the blonde as she went by, making it clear that he had a type. The two women were nearing the young boy, who was still busy investigating the sidewalk, as a black sedan crept from around the corner. "You lookin' for someone, Mannie? Why don't you come in, have a drink? We got any kind of hooch you could want."

The little man's eyes were still in the street and he did not respond to the invitation.

"Mannie, what's the matter..."

The little man, for the first time it seemed, looked at Anthony's face. His reedy voice rose as tires suddenly screeched in the street. "Hey Ton ... I'm *real* sorry ... I just wanted you to know that's the truth..." With that, the little man turned, crouched, and dove as close to the bottom of the Cadillac as he could – scooching his tiny body between the curb and the cars bottom, as Anthony watched, confounded, only the briefest of suspicions beginning to occur to him. Alarms going off inside his head only when the black sedan came skidding to an abrupt halt in front of the store. The windows on that side of the car were down, but still the inside seemed black; the silhouette of a driver seemed without a face. From the shadows of the backseat the mean-looking muzzle of a machine-gun peaked out, and almost instantly erupted; the flash of the blast doing nothing to expose its composer.

A steady stream of slugs tore into – and through, Anthony before his hand was any higher than his waist. His hat and pinky finger were the first things shot off as he went tumbling backwards, spinning as the fusillade went on; the violent chattering of the weapon continuing, deliberately unloading on him until he hit the ground. And then just a few rounds more.

There was only the briefest interval as the compensator rose, drawing its bead on the store. And then the volley began all over again. The long-panned window that made up the stores front burst into a thousand glinting pieces. Dozens and dozens of bottles inside popping like a true shooting gallery. Everyone on the sidewalk hit the ground – whether they'd been shot or not.

For at least another five, eternal seconds the bullets strafed away at the building. Then in an instant it was over; a merciful *clicking* came with the dry fire as the long burst of murder from the car ceased, the sedan screeching away with the same haste in its exit as in its arrival. Its gunning motor growling as it tore up the street.

Few rose immediately. Those that did, noticed there were a few who had not rose at all.

The Big Guns

II

"Get back! Get back, I said!" the uniformed policeman barked at the crowd that had rapidly gathered mass in front of the mangled remains of the Giante liquor store. The grisly sight was perfectly clear from the street – the thrashed bottles and ocean of shattered glass, the ripped apart and slanted shelves of the far wall, nothing in one piece – yet the crowd pushed further. It was still early on the scene, and the border-rope was in the process of being strung up, and until its completion it seemed the duty of crowd-control had fallen to this lone officer, gently waving his flashlight to-and-fro, forcing the crowd back with subtle threats of bludgeoning.

A white wagon pulled away from the scene, skidding and squealing onto Third Street. Not two minutes later a brown flivver came pulling in from the same direction, parking along beside the police cars acting as a sort of barrier that hadn't worked. From the passengers' side a tall man stepped out, the worn heels of his shoes touching the street first. He wore a solid brown suit straight from the rack that clung to bulking shoulders, a matching hat sat above hardened blue-eyes that began examining the scene; just making out a bulging red-stained sheet beyond the heads of the crowd. His granite jaw shifted from side to side in pensive habit. The man from the driver's side came around and joined him. He was just a bit taller. Shoulders just a bit broader. He donned a black suit, not quite made of the same cheap fabric as his companion, yet not quite lavish. He wore a small diamond piece in the center of his maroon tie, yet the most costly of his accessories seemed to be the golden pinky ring he wore on the hand he used to balance a fat cigar in his mouth with each long draw.

The man in the brown suit lead the way, pushing through the crowd, squinting at the sporadic flashes, and even crushing the spent bulbs left by the cameramen and reporters at the peak of their scavenging. "Get back!" The uniform ordered still. "You can snap your pictures and yap about what you don't know from back there, *go on now!*" When the uniform spotted the two stone-faced men pushing his way, his face tightened in frustration. "Look, I just told all these crumbs–"

"I'm Sergeant McGraw, 13th precinct," the man cut in with a hard, grainy voice. His face cold and stoic as he flashed his identification. "This is my partner, Sergeant Reed."

The man in the black suit only continued puffing at his cigar. His glare equally unfeeling.

"Oh. Sure. Go right through, Serg."

And without another word or glance the plainclothesmen pushed past to the core of the scene. Another uniform came loping over to the first one. "You know who that was? That was *Six Shot McGraw!*"

"Who?"

"Six Shot. They call him that on'a count of he buried all six pills of that big boy double action .44 of his into Benny Stanton."

"Benny Stanton, the gangster?" the first policeman said, musing. "You mean ... *that's George McGraw?*"

"Looks like he's back on the street. I recognize his new partner, too. That's Mean Mike Reed. That's quite the pair. Christ, I can't believe they already brought him back."

"Guess they had to." The first policeman now tipped his cap and watched the detectives with the other. "Papers have been making a goddamn true crime hero out of him."

McGraw and Reed made their way through the implicit path, careful to avoid stepping on any unexamined space. Approaching the older uniform, who stood by the bloody, lumpy sheet, McGraw noticed that there was another, just a few yards from the first; the same crimson stains and ominous human impression as its neighbor. Maybe a bit smaller.

The policeman regarded the detectives as they stopped on the other side of the body. "McGraw. Reed."

"Hey, O'Bryan. What's doing?"

"Oh, you know, keepin' the beat. When'd you get back?"

"Eh, I'm like a bad itch — I always creep my way back up." His eyes trailed over the second body down by the curb. "So, give me the works."

"Plenty of witnesses," O'Bryan began. "'Cept nobody saw who was in the car. All say it was a black Ford sedan. Said it was plenty loud. Figure it was souped-up for this kind'a job."

"Plate numbers?"

"Not one, mud or tape or somethin' was coverin' 'em. Everyone gave the same story: Big black car came flying around the corner, stopped abruptly at the store, sprayed it and everyone close, then rabbited out. Everyone dropped when the shootin' started."

"They said the car stopped?"

"That's right. What're you figurin'?"

"Nothing, except it's clear they wanted him dead. Go on."

"The old greaseball next-door was closest. But he ain't talkin'. Those dagos never tell us nothin'. All he said was that they were good boys."

"Would that be the Giantes?" McGraw asked, examining the liquor stores' bullet-riddled moniker.

"That's right. There's two of 'em. This here's Anthony," O'Bryan nudged at the sheet with his foot, "It's the meat wagon for him. He had a .45 automatic under his arm; untouched."

"Is that Sam over there?" Reed finally spoke, cocking his cigar-wielding hand towards the second sheet.

"No. Sam was in the store when it all started, but it didn't do him too much good. He took plenty of lead, but he was still kickin'. Should just about be at St. Mary's by now."

Reed didn't say anything else. He went back to chewing on his fat cigar.

"Then who's that?" McGraw asked grimly.

O'Bryan tipped his cap far back and began to shake his head. "Poor, poor lass. S'shame. Name was Shelly Senter. She'n her friend, Maggie, was on their way to their shift at a diner when these mad dogs came through. Just the damned timing. We had another bus with some boys take the friend over to the hospital, she was in hysterics last I saw'a her. She didn't see nothin' but her friend bein' torn up."

McGraw shook a cigarette loose, spit a flake of tobacco out, and asked O'Bryan a few more questions. He spotted a young man coming in from the street, his rimless-spectacles and baggy suit made him appear too young to be on the force. "What took, Farley? Call came in ten minutes ago."

"You wanted the file on these Giantes, didn't you? Thing was so thick, I only copied some basics and the last decade of their rap-sheets."

"What do you got?"

"Both hustlers. Seems they made a living out of it since grade school. Both released on parole from Stateville earlier this month after a three-year stint on larceny charges. Anthony first, the next week Sam. Brothers owned the liquor store before going under, apparently had family run it while they were away. No parole violations within their short amount of freedom, no known steady girls, no known living associates."

"Living associates?" McGraw repeated, a smoldering cigarette dangling from his mouth.

"That's right. Get this, they were both known members of a now-dead crew called the Turner gang. All six of the then-remaining gang members – brothers excluded – were cut down execution-style in a warehouse uptown, just about a week after the brothers went away."

"Warehouse uptown? You mean the Broad St. Massacre?"

"Exactly. Detectives were sent to the pen to question both brothers due to there known association, but learned exactly nothing. Like you know, the slayings were never solved; chalked up to another gangland hit."

"*Hey you little brats!*" the bellowing voice of the first uniform rang out as the detectives watched him chasing two young boys up the sidewalk.

"*I saw him! I saw him!*" The young blonde boy blurted out straight to McGraw.

"You fink, keep your mouth shut!" his young companion ordered, tugging at his friend's shoulder to no avail.

McGraw looked at the uniform and nodded to the second boy, indicating he wanted him removed. Then McGraw said, "Who, kid? The shooter?"

"No," he cried out, "the third one!"

"What third one?" Reed said, asking only his second question.

"*The third man!* One of them went inside while the other two stayed, then the little one said something to him," the blonde boy pointed without fear to the bloody sheet, "then jumped under that car right before they let loose. Then he went crawling away into that alley!"

"You see his face, kid?"

"Nah, not really. But he was a real shorty. I don't think anyone saw him but us. My pals said I shouldn't talk to you, 'cause you're'a cop. But I says, 'That's Six Shot McGraw, he's alright!'"

"Thanks, kid." McGraw flipped a coin the boys' way before turning back to Farley. "I want you to dig a little more into these Giantes – the latter of the Turner gang too. But first stick around and see if anyone else caught a glimpse of this little man. Go on." When he looked to his partner, Reed was bent down and peaking under the sheet. His face unmoved by whatever remained of Anthony Giante. "Getting pretty juicy, huh?" McGraw said.

"These greaso killings usually are." Reed dropped the sheet and rose. "Doesn't mean much, I don't think. There's always some guy that never gets found. Maybe he was just another poor bastard ducking for cover."

"Maybe." Smoke poured slowly from McGraw's nose as his iron jaw shifted thoughtfully. "But I still wanna find him and ask why he ducked before the shooting started. Let's get to the hospital. I don't want the other brother croaking before we can grill him."

Doctor, Doctor!

III

"Look, I told you, you can't be here." The doctor argued with McGraw as Reed pried for information. With each question, Sam Giante screamed and writhed in his gurney. Though most were in his stomach, he had tiny, congealing holes scattered all over his upper body – one of his earlobes had even been blown off; the mass of bandages that must have been applied on the ambulance ride were sodden with his blood; Reed pressed him nonetheless, speaking in his good ear. "This man will die if we don't operate soon. He might die anyway!"

"The short man. Who is he? *Where* is he?" Reed went on. Giante squirmed in his agony, ignoring the detective. Reed looked to McGraw and shook his head.

"Let's talk away from him, Doc." McGraw led the doctor down the hallway, behind them Reed pulled the privacy curtain shut.

"Look Doc–"

"Listen officer, I mean it. That gentleman is in bad shape, it's a miracle he made it here still breathing, and if he uses any of that breath to answer your questions he'll die."

"I only need two words, Doc. One if that's all I can get. I don't know too much about this guy, except that someone tried pretty hard to kill him – *did* kill his brother – and didn't mind blasting an innocent girl to do it. I need a name or this whole thing might be over already."

As it seemed the doctor might've been considering, a desperate gasp came from behind the curtain. McGraw just beat the doctor down the hall, pulling the curtain to find Reed holding the back of Giante's neck with one hand, grasping his shirt collar with the other; at first glance, it looked quite like he was choking the man. "*Where? Where?*" the detective screamed in his face.

"...C-C-C-Cook ... w-was Cook..." Giante spit out – along with some blood, coating his teeth and lips.

"I know that! *Where is he?*" Reed shook the man somewhat in frustration, seeming not to notice McGraw and the doctor at first. "*Where?*"

"...C-C-C-Cook..." Giante rasped out one last time before his hand fell limply from Reed's wrist, his head lolling back in the detective's hand. He went still.

Reed placed his head back against the pillow as the doctor moved swiftly with his stethoscope, hurrying to Giante's side.

"Cook? How'd you know?" McGraw asked Reed, who'd ambled absently over.

"That's all he kept saying. It was Cook. Cook, Cook, Cook. No address."

The doctor frowned and strung the instrument back around his neck. "Well, sounds like you got that last name. Now will you two please get out of here before someone else peaks your curiosity. Our morgue gets enough business."

Scattered Showers

IV

McGraw hated driving. Especially the kind of driving he was doing now. Weaving in and out of traffic, rounding each curve and turn at high-speed, just managing to keep from veering off the road. No siren to warn other drivers (it was off so as not to alarm Cook). But he was eager to get to Cook's apartment. He didn't blame Reed too much for their delay. He'd known Reed for a while. Since before his suspension for killing a bigshot racketeer, since before he'd been brought back and demoted to Sergeant after being found not guilty of murdering Benny Stanton, since before they'd been partnered up. But he had cut out about five minutes of what McGraw considered valuable time – doing whatever. He hadn't asked; didn't plan to. He figured Reed wouldn't have held them up if it hadn't been important. He might've been in the restroom, or taking an emergency call from one of those ex-wives he was always aching about.

McGraw had called Farley from the hospital immediately after Sam Giante died. Farley did as he was told and had the files ready on everyone named Cook in the county – and two neighboring counties, starting with convicts, and possible members of the Turner gang. The pile they arrived to, proved that Cook was a common name, but Farley had done well and had two separate files waiting. "No one I could find from the Turner's named Cook – not even as an alias." Farley explained. "But I thought about possible connections to the Giantes, and what I found were two different cons who'd served time in Stateville while the Giantes were there: Gregory Cook, released earlier this year after one year for arson; and Emmanuel Cook Jr. released three months ago after five years on B&E charges." Looking at each of the Cook mugshots, McGraw thought Farley would make a decent detective.

It was simple enough to decide which Cook they were after. All they had to do was look at the listed height of five-foot-one Emmanuel Cook Jr. apartment 4D of 223 Martin St. A thirty-four-year old man originally from Brooklyn, New York, who'd been working as a janitor at a recreational center since his release from prison. McGraw went to pull the car around, while Reed did whatever for those five minutes. And then soon they were on their way.

223 Martin St. turned out to be in the heart of the city's tenement section. Each building identical, with a dilapidated, crumbling look. If they were still standing and had four walls, it was near impossible to tell which buildings weren't abandoned. The inside of 223 was dark and depressing, with only the glare of a single naked bulb hanging from the ceiling at each floor. McGraw and Reed made their way to the fourth. Reaching under his arm, McGraw unhooked the strap around the butt of his gun. As far as he was concerned this was a murder suspect they were calling on.

The detectives approached apartment 4D, each of them taking a side of the door; Reed hailed far off, his face concealed under the brim of his hat. McGraw knocked at the door. Nothing. His right hand rested on his belly – where it always did when he began to think of quick-drawing – as he rapped against the door with his left. He knocked at the door again. When there was no answer he started for a third and suddenly the door cracked a few inches. Timid, hazel eyes could be seen just above the doors chain. "Yea?" a sheepish voice inquired.

"Mr. Cook?" McGraw's hand came out of his jacket holding a shiny gold badge. "We're with the police. I'd just like to ask you a few questions, I think you could be a big help to us."

"You're batty if you think I can help you."

"Can we come in?"

"Leave me alone."

"Like I said, I think you can help out. If you can't, I won't waste too much of my time or yours. How 'bout it?"

The dark-eyes fell over the detective, then ran about the hallway. The door closed and was followed by the muffled sound of a rattling chain. It opened all the way this time, and a wiry little man with thinning dark hair and nervous almond-shaped eyes stood before them.

"You said, we?" he asked, before Reed stepped into the doorway with his partner. When he saw him, Cook's eyes looked as though they'd pop out of his skull in an instant. Reed chewed off the end of a cigar and spit the tip out; his eyes cold and unblinking as they set upon Cook. "W-What do you guys want with me! I've done everything I was supposed to!"

"Take it easy, Cook" Reed grunted through clenched teeth. "Like my partner said, we just want to know a few things. No one said you did anything wrong."

Cook's eyes remained glazed with fear. "I-I don't know anything."

"Don't you want to hear the questions first?" McGraw said briskly.

"I just want to be left alone."

McGraw ignored him. "What were you doing at the Giante liquor store this morning?"

If this caught Cook off guard, McGraw didn't see it; Cook's eyes hadn't left Reed since they'd found him. He watched as the detective marched around his apartment, puffing away at his Corona as he examined the shelves, his hands stuffed into his pants pockets with the flaps of his jacket brushed back, the .38 at his waist exposed. "I don't know what you're talking about. I was here all day."

"So, you didn't know Anthony or Sam Giante?"

"No."

McGraw nodded slowly. The way he did when displeased. "How's parole been going, Cook?"

"*Fine!* I've been doing fine," he said, still watching Reed.

"The Giantes didn't quite get a chance to do as well as you. About fifty rounds of .45 slugs made sure of that."

Cook didn't answer.

"Were they not very nice to you in the clink, Cook?" McGraw smirked slyly. "Play a little *too rough* for a fella your size? That what you had against them?"

Cook turned from Reed to McGraw, his face a pale, painful twist of fury and indignation. "Shut up!"

"I don't think anyone could blame you for wanting to cap them if that was the case—"

"*Shut up!*" Cook cried. "You're not gonna pin anything on me!"

McGraw carried on. "—Both Giantes got it. Guess that was the plan though, huh? But how 'bout the girl?"

"What girl?" Cook growled, his attention back on Reed.

"Her name doesn't matter. It might've once, but not anymore. Guess you didn't stick around to see your pals handy work, did you?"

18

"I told you—"

"Going somewhere, Cook?" Reed asked jumping back in, cocking his head toward the direction of a pullout bed, where a half-packed suitcase lay open.

"I-I—"

"You know," McGraw said, "parole violation can be a serious thing; even without a murder-rap to top it off."

Cook's lips curled into a nervous little smile. "No, no, no." He laughed at the end of each word, backing away from McGraw and maneuvering from Reed, who seemed to be circling him. "I wasn't going nowhere! As you guys can see, I don't have much furniture. Where else am I supposed to keep my shirts?" He tittered, hand trembling as he worked a cigarette into his mouth; he was by the bed now, pulling one shirt after the other out of the suitcase. "See, just my shirts..." This was when Cook turned so that his back blocked-off sight of the bed. McGraw, jaw shifting, watched as Cook's short arm plunged deeper into the suitcase; exploring blindly, groping for something.

Before he could think of doing any different, McGraw shoved his unwary partner across the room, spilling his cigar and hat; Reed hit the wall and crashed behind a dresser as Cook spun around on the detectives, a tiny black automatic in his hand. He let a shot loose, the bullet ripping past McGraw as he dove to his own side of the room, right hand traveling up his belly and under his arm as he went. Cook was already darting into the short hallway in his apartment; Reed — up and with the program by now — unsheathed his .38 and fired twice as he trailed the little man, missing each shot and shattering a window with one.

McGraw, back on his feet, cannon in hand, followed Reed toward the hall. They could just see the door closing. McGraw started forward, but Reed pulled him back. McGraw looked to his partner and saw his index finger against his mouth. Not understanding, McGraw took another step, and heard the shrill, muffled voice on the other side of the door.

"...What ... What're you doing here ... No, no I did everything I was supposed to ... No!"

Reed took his partner by the collar and yanked him back. McGraw was behind cover not a second before a burst of machine-gun fire came tearing through the door, ripping away at the panels; the force of the volley splintering and spitting large, varying pieces of wood out into the hall. A river of lead flew past the detectives and tore into the far wall. McGraw watched the sinuous streaks of holes being drilled into the plaster; the wild, vertical patterns told him the shooter was dipping the machine-gun up and down as he unloaded.

Soon the shooting ceased. There was a dull thud from the other side of the door – quickly followed by footsteps, and as McGraw peaked around the corner he could see a figure disappear past the ragged, spiked mass of holes in the door. Keeping low, he dashed into the hall; Reed followed close. The door was unlocked, but there was dead weight on the other side. McGraw looked through the hole and saw the bloody legs and feet at the foot of the door. He rammed it with his shoulder and the body tumbled lithely as McGraw came in low, his sights set down the eight-inch barrel of his Smith & Wesson, covering the empty room. The billowing drape at an open window caught his attention, and he sprung as Reed entered the room.

Cannon first, McGraw peaked out of the window and down the fire escape; the figure was moving with such haste the stairs shook as McGraw climbed out onto them. Skipping two stairs at a time McGraw caught flashes of a white hat through the stairs and could see that the man was already to the first floor.

Bending as far as he dared over the rails, McGraw took aim and blasted at the bottom of the staircase the man (whose face was masked under the wide brim of his fedora) was half-through descending. The slug ricocheted off the second-to-last step, sparking and sending the man stumbling backwards – McGraw could actually see the Tommy slip from hands as he tripped up, but before he could shoot again the man was crawling back up the stairs, and out of clear sight; the foregrip and Cutts compensator of the machine-gun disappearing with him, creeping up the stairs seemingly on its own.

And then lead poured from below, the sound of bullets bouncing all around him were more deafening than the blast of the weapon spitting them out. All McGraw could do was back against the railing and cover his face. He felt a slash across his temple and collapsed as the sound of dry fire came. Pulling himself up with blood already seeping into one eye he saw a man in a white hat and black overcoat scurrying across the street, a Tommy gun cradled in his arms. A black sedan waiting for him.

McGraw sent a shot across the street; the impact of the large caliber bullet seemed to slam the car door shut after the man had already crawled inside. Rubber screamed as the sedan pulled into the street. McGraw aimed for the tire, vision blurred by his own blood. He saw the bullet drill through the top of the passengers' door; the shadow of the driver hopped a foot in his seat; the bullet must have planted itself beside him. A shot blared out from above; Reed had made it down the fire escape. McGraw didn't see Reed's shot land, but *his* fourth and final one blew out the back window as the car sped off, swerving and disappearing around the closest corner.

The echoing of the cars' motor faded quickly, the city silence deaf-like for the two detectives. McGraw gazed gravely at the street corner, his jaw jutting.

"Jesus, George!" Reed exclaimed seeing his partner's face.

"I'm alright," McGraw grumbled, accepting a handkerchief and splotching around his eye. "What took you?"

"You didn't expect me to stick my head out the window when that lead-storm started, did you?"

"You were still inside then?"

"Thought I'd see how well Cook could soak up slugs."

"Hell, I could've told you not to bother. He got the same dose as the Giantes. 'Cept he got it point blank."

"I'll put in the call," said Reed.

McGraw watched the corner a minute longer. Traffic in the street had resumed as though there hadn't just been a shooting. Any potential witnesses who could've provided a description of the gunman moved along; as though it hadn't been enough for McGraw that they'd braked so successfully, not running the gunman down in the street. He spilled the spent casings of his .44 revolver, replaced them, snapped the cylinder shut, and stuck the gun back under his arm. After that he started back up the fire-escape to clean up what was left of their only lead.

Blood on the Curb

Curb

Part Two

Big Chief Undger

I

Another murder scene. Another machine-gun killing. This time the police had even been present for it and had been able to do exactly nothing about it. Emmanuel Cook Jr. – the only lead in the Giante liquor store slaying, which had resulted in the death of two brothers (both ex-cons who'd done time with Cook) with ties to an old gang who'd been cut down in a gangland massacre, and a young, innocent woman whose biggest mistake in life was not being early or late for work that morning – lay dead in his own apartment, full of the same brand of .45 slugs that had raked the Giante storefront. Cook was still slumped against the open door when the first responding unit arrived, less than fifteen minutes after the shooting. The macabre scene of the little man's bullet-riddled body, overwhelmed with tiny, coagulated holes peppered about his face and torso, proved to be the perfect atmospheric shot of brutality and apparent force of gangsterism the unnamed detectives had allegedly allowed; the few camera-vultures and ink-pushers that were somehow permitted to be there ate it up. Bulbs flashed and smashed, and questions flew.

Soon a burly man sauntered into the apartment. An imposing figure – standing at nearly six-five, even with hunched shoulders. Below eyes that held a lurking fury – along with a flicker of something enigmatic – a thick mustache, that may have once been a feathered-brown, was now streaked with the same iron-gray present at his temples. The thick heels of his Oxfords resounding with purpose in each step; an air of draconian authority in his stride. More cameras went off as he entered the room and studied the body. "Chief! Chief!" the reporters called out.

"Chief Undger, is this a mob-killing?"

"Chief, is this related to the drive-by shooting this morning?"

"Chief, is there a new gun in town to take Stanton's place? Was this killing some sort of message? Is Detective McGraw working the case?"

"They got their pictures, get them out of here," the chief snarled sonorously to a uniform who promptly directed the pack of newsmen out into the hallway.

When they were out of the room and the door was shut the Chief said, "Where are they?"

None of the officers answered him.

"I said, where the hell are McGraw and Reed?"

Finally, a young uniform braved-up and said, "They weren't here Chief. We don't know where they are."

Just then the door opened, and another uniform came rushing in, the cameras of reporters who'd been absent minutes before flashed behind him in a desperate attempt for a shot of the mangled little man, retreating only when they realized the policeman would close the door on their arms if they didn't pull back. The officer leaned over Chief Undger's shoulder, and spoke low, "Chief, we just found a wagon burning in an abandoned lot off Berkley that fits the description of the car from the Giante drive-by. It's even got a few bullet holes and empty shells casings inside."

"Any word form McGraw?"

"McGraw? No."

The Chief puckered his lips and rubbed at his forehead. When he spoke, each word rose with his agitation. "Find them. *Find them. FIND THEM!*"

Early Retirement

II

WHEN THEIR ONLY LEAD was torn to pieces, and after McGraw narrowly avoided the slab himself, there was little time to act. Reed had done just as he'd said and phoned the station. A responding unit would be there soon; also, the Chief wanted to see them, he was on his way, too. McGraw started rifling through Cook's drawers and suitcase, dismissing Reed's questioning and recommendations of stopping to clean the blood from his face. There was no time for that thanks to Reed. He knew the only time the Chief ever wanted to see him personally was when he had something he could lay into him about. Finding nothing, he started digging into the dead-man's pockets, ignoring the extra blood he was getting on his cheap-suit sleeves. Tossing aside most of the contents – including a pack of Chesterfields and nine-dollars and some change, he came across a book of matches from a hotel called the *Reserve*; inside the book, in quick-hand scrawl, read *ROOM 235*.

"You coming or not?" was all McGraw had to say when Reed began to almost insist that they stay and wait for the Chief, saying they'd only bury themselves deeper in shit if they kept on this way. He only conceded when McGraw turned his back and started off without him.

"Alright, alright, you stubborn bastard. But I'm driving, use those extra handkerchiefs in the compartment and clean yourself up."

The manager of the *Reserve* was a short, sheik-looking fellow with huge spectacles who, at the sight of the detectives and their shields, immediately insisted they provide a warrant before searching any of his rooms; capriciously changing his mind only after a cold-eyed stare-down from a man he soon recognized from the papers as "Six Shot McGraw." They found nothing in room 235, except a still burning cigarette left behind in the ashtray, and a drink with ice that had only just begun to melt. They learned from the manager that there were two men, each had checked themselves in under the name of Smith, claiming to be brothers who'd left the hotel in a hurry only ten minutes before. McGraw cursed out loud and asked the manger to describe these "Smiths." The description he gave was quite vague, however one detail he included was useful enough: one of the Smiths, donned a white hat that was always cocked at a rakish angle.

They gathered a few more facts about the "Smiths" brief and uneventful stay at the Reserve, and, after making it clear to the manager what would happen to him if either of the "Smiths" returned and he did not inform them, left for the station.

The inside of Precinct 13 was a palpable atmosphere of solemn discomfort; each detective and uniform nodded respectfully as McGraw made his way out of the station bathrooms. He'd already had Doyle, a fellow Sergeant and former army medic, patch up the slash above his eye, and he changed from his blood-stained clothes to a clean shirt and black jacket (that didn't quite match his brown hat or trousers) that he kept in his locker. He found Reed waiting at his desk, but before he could open his mouth the Chief emerged from his imperial cave of an office and barked out in front of the entire room, "*McGraw! Reed!* Get the hell in my office!"

Instead of meeting McGraw's gaze, Reed lit a cigar, shrugged, and started into the office. McGraw loosened his tie even more and followed.

Chief Undger loomed over the seated detectives from the other side of his desk. "You should've checked in with me before you followed through with this lead. This Cook thing might've been prevented. Now, where are we? One dead parolee, and God knows how many murderers free. No closer to knowing anything about this morning's shooting."

"Look Chief," said McGraw, "I've never had to ask permission to poke around before – especially when it comes to a killing and some trigger-happy birdies on the loose with a fifty-round typewriter, and I don't see why I should've in this case. We have good reason to believe that Emmanuel Cook was the third man spotted at the liquor store this morning, and *just* as good a reason to believe he was in on the shooting."

"Good reason?" the Chief scoffed, no humor in his face, all his attention on McGraw. "You mean that so-called witness of yours? Some gutter-punk who spends his school days on a street corner? *HA!* How reliable can you possibly believe that to be?"

"Considering he was standing just a few feet down the sidewalk when the whole thing went down, I'd say pretty goddamn reliable," McGraw said matter-of-factly, slipping a cigarette into his mouth.

Chief Undger's lips pursed, then tightened. His face flush with anger. Detective Reed sat quietly, smoking his cigar with his ring hand, observing the exchange.

"And we're not exactly where we started on this thing either, Chief. I saw this guy; not his face, but his build and dress. Watched him climb into the same Ford described at the Giante scene. Managed to find out where he and his pal had been staying, and got the same description of the birdie in the white hat."

"You got a description of an outfit that fits Capone's and every other half-ass wanna-be wiseguy like him!" the Chief continued his rebuke as McGraw ran a match across the bottom of his shoe; only he didn't bring the flame to the cigarette in his mouth. His eyes were hard on the Chief's pointing finger.

The Chief saw this, drew his hand back and ran his sweating palms against his trousers. "You're off the case, both of you."

McGraw's eyes trailed back to Undger's. He dropped the match and snapped the cigarette in his mouth, speaking incredulously. "What's that?"

"As far as I'm concerned this was just another gangland hit. Scumbags killing scumbags. Can't even say for sure they're related because of the way you went about it."

McGraw's face took on an even colder demeanor, but he said nothing. Though it was Undger speaking, Reed's attention was firmly on his partner.

"We get a couple of these shootings every week. Oh, I'll admit it was rather unfortunate about that young girl getting caught up in it. But if you look at history you'll see that's *nothing* in comparison. Hell, you should have seen how many civilians got it the first year the hoodlums got hold of a Tommy gun. No, there are too many more promising cases that need working to let this mess go on. It's partly my own fault, it was too soon to let you back on the job, McGraw. You're still caught up in that Stanton killing. Reed even said that kid-witness of yours recognized you as "Six Shot McGraw." How're you supposed to move on to the next case when the public won't let you out of the last. Now I'm not saying that you're entirely to blame, just that—"

30

"Alright, that's enough," McGraw said gruffly, standing fast enough that his chair went rocking precariously on its back legs. One hand was buried deep in his pants pocket, holding his jacket flap back so that his magnum, sheathed in its leather shoulder-holster, showed clearly. His other hand outstretched, index finger aimed at Chief Undger in a mirroring way. "I don't know why you're jumping down my throat on this thing – at first, I thought it was because of the heat I brought down when I popped Stanton, but now I'm not so sure. Yea. Yea, I plugged that crumb; it happened just the way the board said it did, too. I shot him down because no one else would, and every time we made a move on him he'd buy his way out of it, thumbing his nose at us as his shyster lawyer walked him out of the jailhouse. Now, I looked the other way when you tried talking the commissioner out of reinstating me, I even let it go when you got me demoted to Sergeant – but now you're trying to hang the death of a murder suspect on me because I was there looking for answers? *HA!*" He barked the Chief's nasty, humorless little laugh back and went on. "Look here, Undger. Whoever that birdie was in Cooks apartment was ready and waiting for him. I don't know if he'd already been there, or if he snuck in the window while we were grilling Cook, but it's clear enough that the little guy was a dead-man walking, and that he knew it, too. Yea, it's tough we couldn't have done more, but there wouldn't have been an opportunity to do anything else except clean up the mess if I'd done it your way and stopped to ask you to hold my hand. And as far as it being over, you're right." McGraw's hand shot into his jacket as though he were drawing on the Chief, instead brushing over the butt of his gun and coming back out with his golden badge. He let it clunk against Undger's desk and turned for the door.

Reed finally stood and spoke. "Now hold on a second, George. Let's not lose our heads on this thing. You're taking this all way too personally."

"Bullshit," McGraw snarled. "And I felt bad about being suspicious of you; thinking it was strange how you seemed to be going out of your way to slow our roll down on this thing but putting it off as incompetence. Well now I know. When'd you get a chance to talk to Undger about the kid, Mike?" McGraw's brows rose, Reed recognized the familiar slick gesture as something McGraw would do to a suspect. "Was it after we got Cook's address? Did you not know where he was before that? And I've got kind of a hard time believing you didn't mention to Undger where we were going. Was he the only one you told?"

Reed only stared at first. His dark, beady eyes lost whatever affability had been in them. "Don't go stepping too far, George. We've both got shields, we've always gotten along. Why should that end because a couple of hoods got mowed down? You of all guys should feel that those mutts had it coming."

McGraw had fished out another cigarette, managing to light this one. He drew a deep breath of smoke in, letting it pour from his nostrils as he looked to his former partner. His eyes colder than ever before, but his voice noncommittal. "Mike ... I don't know why you've been shrugging off our leads all day... I don't know why you had to stop to fill Undger in about what we knew before we went to Cooks – and I'm not sure why he's making out like he didn't know..." McGraw's gaze only briefly fell over Undger at this point; searing stares of contempt passing between the two. "...And I don't know how that gunzo made it there when he did, as if he'd learned where he was going the same time we did ... But I know that if I think about it too hard, I might come up with something I don't want to know...

That's the biggest reason it's over. I might be known as the guy who goes around capping gangsters, but there's at least one *big* difference in this whole set-up, Mike. And now that I know you can't see it – or maybe just don't care ... It's better that I'm not in this picture." McGraw turned his back to Reed then, opening the door.

From behind his desk, Unger called out, "What about your gun, McGraw!"

"Fuck off, Undger! The cannon is mine." And with that, McGraw left the Chief's office.

Truth and Trouble

III

He'd found an empty box and was scooping the few personal affects out of his desk; mostly notebooks and a couple boxes of .44 shells. Word had already spread through the stationhouse, and cops would come in odd pairs from time to time to shake his hand or say goodbye. McGraw seemed at peace enough about his decision; at least, as peaceful as he could be. Eventually Farley came along, a big dumb smile on his face until he saw McGraw's head. "What happened to you, Serg?"

McGraw frowned. "Someone didn't like my face, tried to rearrange it. Where the hell you been, Farley?"

"You told me to keep digging into these Giantes. Well I struck gold." He dropped his file, opened it to a bookmarked page, and, adjusting his glasses, ran a finger along each line he reported. Starting with the zinger. "There are *three* Giante brothers, not two."

McGraw stuck a cigarette in the corner of his mouth and sat down. "Yea?"

"There's Sam, the oldest. Anthony, the middle child. And Charlie, the youngest. Didn't come up with the other records I pulled before, because apparently, when Charlie got out of prison three years ago he got married and took his wife's last name in an attempt to go straight; from what I've found on him since the discovery, seems like it stuck. Not a lick of trouble since."

"'Till now, maybe," McGraw grumbled, cigarette dangling. "What's the new name?"

35

"Carlo. Charlie Carlo. Address: 583 Broughton Street."

Smoke poured out in a rapid plume as McGraw's jaw shifted pensively. He smiled, shook his head, silently cursing and muttering something inaudible, then crushed his cigarette in the tray. "You're a prince, Farley," he said putting on his hat and jacket and starting outside.

From behind, Farley called, "You going to catch up with Reed? He just started out with Undger."

Without looking back, McGraw hollered over his shoulder, "No. I don't work here anymore."

And with that bit of perplexity, he left Farley to stand there at his empty desk, looking around questioningly and asking around without receiving answers, "What the hell happened?"

~ ~ ~

McGraw found a shell of a woman at 583 Broughton; the lady who answered the door and nodded timidly when asked "Mrs. Carlo?" was of a sickly pallor, with heavy lines at her mouth, and dark, sagging bags hanging under drab eyes. She wasn't exactly short, but seemed smaller with the slouched shoulders and baggy, disheveled clothing. Yet beneath it all McGraw got the impression that she must have once been pretty and sweet enough to convince a career criminal – born of career criminals – to change his very way of living.

"My name is George. George McGr–"

"You're another screw," she said, gritting her teeth. "I can see that plainly. You've got that smug, heartless look in your eye, and that condescending way of speech. Go away, I've nothing more to say to your kind!"

McGraw slipped his foot in the door before she could close it and continued speaking to her through the crevice. "If we're speaking frankly to each other, Mrs. Carlo, then I might as well tell you now that I'm not a flattie anymore. Just a curiously concerned citizen."

Her stoic mask of strength yielded, and she broke down into her hands, turning from the open door and letting McGraw walk inside. "What's the matter with you people? Why can't you just leave him alone? Charlies been square ever since he got out of that concrete-coffin!"

"I've no reason to doubt that," McGraw said, not quite believing it. "But I think that something from his past might be coming back to bite. Something he and his brothers must have done or been involved in while he was still a player. Whatever the reason, Mrs. Carlo, it's pretty clear that the other party is cleaning house and that Charlie needs help."

The lines at her mouth deepened downward as her lips tightened shut.

"Where's your husband?"

"I don't know."

McGraw nodded slowly, jaw shifting.

"You're one of them ... I can tell..."

"Yea, you said that already," McGraw muttered impatiently, crossing the room and selecting a cigarette.

"I don't just mean a cop. You're one of *those* cops. Like your friends who were just here."

McGraw yanked the cigarette from his mouth and steadied his glare back on the woman. "How's that?"

"Sure, I can tell. You're hard, like they were. When they came here I thought one of them was a gangster, until he showed me his badge." She brought two fingers to her mouth and actually spat between them, onto her own carpet, and cursed in Italian. *"Dog Catchers!"*

She didn't notice that McGraw was groping behind himself for the window seal. He found support and forced his voice into its' natural guttural state. "What did he look like?"

"Who?"

"*Who?*" he mocked. "*Who* the fuck do you think? The fucking cop, what did he look like?"

She doubled back as he barked at her. "I ... he ... he was tall ... wore a red tie ... I don't know ... and a pinky ring!"

Suddenly he couldn't think straight. His world had become a blurry, confusing suggestion of the worst. There were suspicions before, sure – but nothing like now.

She was still sobbing, still talking. "...he'll never forgive me! Never..."

"What? What're you talking about?"

"Charlie! Charlie will never forgive me!" she blurted, the moisture of her eyes glinting, the tears causing her light shade of make-up to run in black, morbid streaks. "I had to tell them! *I had to!* They promised me they only wanted to help him! That they wanted to keep him safe! I was so tired of the hiding and sneaking around, and I knew he'd never go to the police himself!"

"What did you say? Hurry up, tell me!"

She collapsed into a chair and cried, "I told them where Charlie is hiding! I had to, they said they'd help! What was I to do? They were the police..." She went back to weeping into her palms, but McGraw took her by the shoulders and shook her.

"Where is he? Where? *Where?*"

"The Beltone!" she cried, panting between the words. "The Beltone ... under Ralph Goodis..."

McGraw pushed himself up and made for the door. Behind him, Mrs. Carlo called out, "I had to! He wouldn't tell me anything, but I know that he's in danger! I heard about those brothers of his! I was so scared, I thought he'd gone crazy; saying people were after him! That it wasn't safe for me if he was home! That he was being followed by, by, men in white hats!"

Knock, Knock

IV

"But I have told you, monsieur has specifically requested not to be disturbed by anyone – even our hotel staff. I'm afraid it's out of the question," the Beltone manger explained to McGraw from behind the desk. It was a pretty small joint. Brownstone front, five stories, six rooms each floor. The barren lobby echoed voices of tension throughout a wooden room, adorned in dozens of hunting trophies; plaques engraved with detailed accounts of the kill were nailed below each of the severed heads of boars and bucks.

"Look froggy, this is important. I'm a cop, got it? This guy is a dangerous criminal."

The manager eyed him over suspiciously. "Let me see your badge."

McGraw smiled, nodding his head. "Ok." He reached inside of his jacket and came back out holding his magnum. He thumbed the hammer back and let the tiny Frenchmen observe the cylinder spin. "This is my badge, see?"

"Wi. Wi," the manager agreed vigorously, flipping through the hotel registration. As his finger ran about the page, McGraw noticed the framed map of the hotel layout on the wall behind him.

"Room 9, Monsieur. Second floor."

"That's an adjoining room, isn't it?"

~ ~ ~

The adjoining room proved the Beltone was a flophouse if there ever was one. A single, almost cot-like bed was situated against the far wall in the middle of the tight room. A metal chair that didn't match the desk it was with was the rooms only other furnishment. Charlie Carlo had been cautious about the adjoining room, as the manager told McGraw how he'd paid extra for the use of both rooms. He'd even tried purchasing the skeleton-key, so no one could get in with it. The manager said he'd denied its' existence despite the enticing offer, but somehow McGraw had been more persuasive, and he handed it over after being warned that alerting the local police about what was happening now would only lead to a gunfight in his hotel. McGraw had used the key to slink into the room. For the first twenty minutes or so he stayed on his toes. He'd been certain that he would arrive too late; again, only able to clean up the mess. But after the first half-hour he moved the chair in front of the door and sat down to listen. From the other side of the door McGraw could hear Charlie Carlo's pacing and nervous tweaks with the radios volume.

By the third hour the sun was beginning to set, and the room grew darker. McGraw had gone through half a pack of cigarettes and three ponies from a bottle he'd found in the desk drawer next to the Gideon. As he gave into the fourth, shadows suddenly lingered from under the door to the hall. The figures paused at his door, and McGraw drew his gun and took silent aim that way. Soon the shadows kept on; McGraw held his sights on them as they disappeared from the crack of the door, to presumably where they were sauntering by on the other side of the wall. He stood, and carefully maneuvered by the door to the adjoining room, mindful not to cast his own shadow. Through the thin wood piece and over the steady, muffled swing music, he could hear bits and pieces of what transpired: Like the abrupt opening of a door and the screeching of chair legs, and the word, "*...Oh...*"

"*...Hello Giante,*" said a voice that sent a cold surge up McGraw's back. "*...Just take it easy, now. Don't make any fast moves...*"

McGraw gently thumbed back the hammer of his revolver, as a third voice – this one, though deep and full of dominance, he found rather pestiferous - told Charlie Giante to stand still while he frisked him.

"*...L-Look... I'm out of it, ok?... I've been out of it since...*" much of the sentence was cut out by the ritzy clarinet solo from the radio, but the end of it was clear enough. "*...you've already killed my brothers. Both of them...*"

"*...Relax Giante,*" the first voice said. "*...We're just here on a friendly call. Never mind the heaters. Here, we'll put 'em away. Feel better?*"

McGraw didn't hear an answer from the third, strange voice.

The first went on. "*...All we want is to get a few things clear... Now, what did your brothers tell you before they died?*"

There was only silence from the room then, but someone must have made a convincing gesture to Giante because soon enough he was speaking. "*...Nothing... They didn't tell me a thing... Except... Except that they knew you hadn't forgotten about them... They heard about O'Neal and Frost from inside the Can. They knew better than anyone else what really happened... What they thought would*" *happen to them... I thought they were crazy... until... until..."*

The second voice: *"...Go on, you crumb..."*

"... You hacks are more murderous than any of us ever were! You think it matters if you don't pull the trigger personally?"

"...Now don't go getting excited, Giante..." said the first voice. *"...I don't want to have to take my rod back out... Then we can see how personal you want to get about it..."*

McGraw couldn't be certain, but it sounded like a sob might have escaped the final Giante. *"...Please..."* he begged, *"...please... I've been out of it for years... I'd forgotten all about you until they got out... Please, I have a wife now!"*

"...That's swell. That's real swell," the first voice went on in a patronizingly playful tone. *"... I've had a few of those myself. Don't expect any medals for it... And don't worry so much, Giante. I told you we're not going to hurt you... We'll be leaving in just a minute now... But before we go I want you to dig deep, real deep, understand? Dig deep in that noggin of yours and think... is there anyone else out there who knows about us? All of us... Anyone at all? Think hard now..."*

The skeleton key McGraw had lifted off the manager had been resting in the keyhole to the next room for hours, and now, gripping it delicately, he shifted his feet into a ready, stealthy position, careful to move on the balls of his feet to avoid creaking floorboards, mindful that the long-barrel of his gun didn't knock against the door.

"... *I told you, I'm out if it... I wouldn't know if there was...*"

A minute passed, presumably so the uninvited guests could contemplate the authenticity of the answers they were receiving, and then there were footsteps. "...*It's ok, Giante... I believe you... it's ok, don't worry anymore... just stay here, we'll let ourselves out...*"

With no finesse, McGraw twisted the key, then the knob, and kicked the door open. The gun at his waist led the way into the room. "No!" he ordered. "Stay awhile."

In the little room he'd pounced into, McGraw spotted a swarthy, dark-haired man sitting on the same shabby bed he'd had in the next room; his eyes were the size of half-dollars and full of fear. It was clear he thought he was about to be murdered. McGraw had passed a quick, inspecting glance over the stranger he knew to be Charlie Giante, but his dictations and gun were aimed on the pair by the rooms entrance. There, on the other side of the room, frozen in incredulity and chagrin, were Chief Undger and Detective Mike Reed. Their mouths gaping, their hands looming by their beltlines.

"McGraw!" Undger snarled, whipping back into his natural, authoritative state. "What is the meaning of this? Not only are you not an officer of the law anymore, but you're holding two high-ranking men

45

who are at gunpoint! What the hell's gotten into you?"

"Shut up," McGraw said drily. He was staring at Reed, but not speaking to him directly. "Come on back in, boys. That's it, nice 'n easy. We're going to have a little chat."

"McGraw, there's a time and a place for this, and this isn't it," Reed said, almost pleading with him subtly.

"I'm sorry, I meant Mr. Giante and I are going to have a chat." Keeping his gunsights on his former coworkers he turned his attention to the man on the bed. "Hello Charlie. We've never met, but I bet you know what I want to hear about, don't you?"

The stranger said nothing. His eyes ran about one man to the next. Perplexity seemed to have replaced a certain amount of his fear.

"McGraw, you'll do time for this!" Undger growled. "And I'll see that you do every bit of it in the dungeons with the schizos and the queers!"

"Undger, if you say one more word I'll blow your kneecap off. And you know with this cannon, you'd never walk right again." He said this with no hostility, only a matter-of-factness. The eight-inch barrel of his .44 slanted at a downward angle, and though the Chief swayed nervously in place, the muzzle of the gun followed.

"Don't do this, George," Reed implored one last time, "these heels aren't worth the trouble you're going to. None of them."

McGraw said nothing to his former partner. Only nodded his head up and down slowly, shifting his jaw in that old, pensive habit. When he spoke to Giante, he spoke from the side of his mouth. "Come on, spill! Who killed your brothers and Cook? How do these mugs tie into it?"

"I... I don't know..."

Look now, there's no tim-"

"But I don't know *who* actually did it!" he insisted. "Some hired guns I suppose." He glared at the two officers then. "They don't do their own dirty work."

"Then how about the next question? How about the why?"

A sort of croak came out of Undger then, but whatever words were working their way out were stifled by the inch or two McGraw raised his gun when he heard it.

"Why?" Giante repeated. "Why? You're saying you really don't know *why*?"

"Cut the dramatics and get to the facts."

"Here's a fact: Along with two other former detectives – who are also dead – your pals over there are responsible for killing six people in cold blood!

And that was three years ago. That numbers been going up recently."

"Six people? What're you..." McGraw's words fell short. His eyes trailed back up to the officers he held at gunpoint. Undger's eyes were fixed on the floor, but Reed met his solemn gaze. "You don't mean... the Turner gang... the Broad St. Massacre?"

"That's exactly what I mean. Before the Chief over there became a big shot, he was just another cheap badge on the take, along with Reed and two others named O'Neal and Frost. Two years ago, O'Neal and Frost were indicted on corruption charges and these two were certain they'd sing for leniency. They handled it the only way they know... and it looked like a drug bust gone bad, alright. But that's only because they had the triggermen plant the junk there for the cops to find!"

"YOU SHUT YOUR GODDAMN MOUTH, YOU MISERABLE SONOFA-"

Before another word could pass Undger's lips there was a deafening explosion in the room, and the Chief's leg buckled under him after chunks of flesh and bone burst from his leg. He crumpled to the floor, crying and cursing McGraw. *"My knee! My knee, you fuck! You fuck, I'll be a fucking cripple!"*

Reed took a step away, closer to the bed. McGraw only looked back to Giante. The stare was enough, and the last Giante brother went on with his story. "I-I-It was always to shut someone up. They had the boys in the warehouse killed because after they refused to supply us with anymore pinched-dope without raising the prices, this fellow named Yorke – our leader, I

48

guess – got it in his mind to tell them that we not only wouldn't pay more for it, but that we'd spill the juice about what they were up to their copper buddies, if they didn't hand the stuff over for nothing. None of us thought it was smart, but before anything could happen word got back to those four about it, and that was apparently enough to have everyone clipped. My brothers and I would've been in the ground a lot sooner if we hadn't been locked-up at the time. And now ... I guess my brothers were just loose ends to something that was supposed to be over. I never knew Cook, but Anthony and Sam mentioned him plenty in their letters. Said he was on the level."

"They used their pal Cook to lure them out for the killing," McGraw said disgustedly, revelation in his voice.

"It was more complex than that, George," Reed said, speaking above Undger's cries. "It's *always* more complex than that. You should know that better than anyone! Why else would you have knocked-off Stanton the way you did? We did what we needed. And sure, we used their own to take care of it. Why not? They do it for sport every day, so what if we kept police safe by using button-men? They all get it soon enough anyway. We did exactly what we're supposed to do: We stopped violent criminals. We looked out for our own. Period." Reed had begun to saunter McGraw's way. "Just listen to the details, George. You'll see things clearly when you hear how it really was." He stood in front of his former partner, grinning amiably.

McGraw's jaw stopped moving, and soon his lips curled in a strange, receptive smile. He began to laugh. It began as a light snicker but grew into a hearty chuckle. He laughed and looked at each man in the room. Reed hesitated but joined in. Giante only watched in bewilderment; not understanding anything anymore. Even Undger had managed to lessen his sobs to observe McGraw. The laughter died down, and soon McGraw lowered his pistol. With his free hand, still tittering here-and-there, he fished out his pack and offered it toward Reed; who smiled and accepted a cigarette.

The second he pulled it free McGraw brought the butt of his gun up, rapping it against Reed's jaw. The detective toppled backwards, tripped against the bedpost, and collapsed onto the floor, unconscious.

Then McGraw turned his attention to Undger. Taking slow, deliberate paces his way. "You *louse*," he growled, "You yellow, weaseling, *louse*. I ought to..."

BANG BANG

With the knock at the door everyone who was awake froze. **BANG BANG**; another knock.

"Expecting company?" McGraw kicked Undger, then looked to Giante. "Slid under the bed. Keep quiet and stay put."

BANG BANG

He fixed back on Undger. A vicious grin spreading across his face. "You really weren't going to hurt him, were you? No, no, you've got special friends with fancy toys to do that business for you. Well, let's see if they'll do it for me."

"*McGraw, no!*"

Another knock, McGraw sheathed his pistol and his powerful hands fell over Chief Undger, covering his mouth and dragging him up and to the door. He took a big step aside, and, keeping the latch hooked-on, he jerked the door open, giving it the impression of being answered. In that same instant he stomped Undger in his bad leg and leapt back.

The Chief straightened in agony, hopping on his good leg desperately, screaming, "*Don't! It's me!*" But bullets were already shredding past the door and ripping into Undger. He hit the floor, but the volley went on a second longer. His friends were giving him the same through-the-door special they'd given Cook. His corpse tumbled around in different grisly poses until the shooting ceased.

McGraw drew his pistol back out and jumped over the Chief's mangled body, stomping the worn heels of his shoes as loud as he could. As he made it to archway of the adjoining room he turned back. The butchered door was creeping open, the chain shot off in the hail of gunfire. A machine-gun muzzle was peeking into the room. McGraw fired a shot, slamming the door shut on the weapon, then he dashed into his room. Cursing himself for locking his own rooms door, he unlocked it, flung it open, and leapt into the hallway, where he peered around and saw a pudgy little man dressed in black; a yellow bow-tie where his neck should have been. He had a snub-nose revolver in his hand.

"Out here, out here!" the small gunman's reedy voice blurted into Giante's room.

McGraw shot at him. Clipping the doorway just above the man's shoulder as he dove for cover. That was when the volley came ripping through the wall of McGraw's room, narrowly missing him as he tripped up and fell backwards. The bullets kept on, and odd bits of plaster spilled down onto him. He regained his feet and made for the staircase nearby. Before he could take his first step down, a shot rang out from behind, and suddenly his leg gave out from under him.

McGraw went crashing down the stairs, the sound of his own head pounding at each step echoing throughout the narrow, wooden staircase. He smashed into the wall at the first-floor landing, then began groping around frantically for his pistol. He could hear the footfalls coming from above. He spotted the gun at the second to last step and pounced on top of it. He juggled it in his hands, fumbling for a proper grasp as he drew a bead on the crown of a white fedora peaking from the second floor. A nasty-looking man with a pointy, slanted-nose like a vulture, and face full of scars came out sneering and blasting away with the Tommy gun in his arms.

McGraw rolled on the landing, avoiding the stream of shots that ran up the wall behind him, and unloaded his final three rounds back to back in a panic. The first shot missed completely, digging into the ceiling, but the second went up through the gunman's chin and out the top of his head and into the ceiling next to the other; his head rocked stupidly, and he gave a death-grip squeeze of the trigger and released another wild volley of gunfire. But the third shot struck his chest and he bumped off the post and fell onto the railing, sliding down by his torso toward McGraw while still somehow holding onto the stockless-machine-gun; until his body crashed against the post at the bottom of the stairs. The smoking weapon gave a resounding thud as it toppled down one stair to the next, an acute slowness in its' every decent.

McGraw fired twice more at the folded body before he realized his gun was empty – then he heard the resonating voice of the pugnacious gunman from above, shots coming between each threat. "I'll kill ya! (**bang!**) I'll kill ya, you sonofabitch (**bang!**)! I'll kill ya! I'll kill ya (**bang!**)!"

McGraw felt the last shot whiz by as he dove down the final stair-set in a reckless attempt to land on the Tommy gun. He felt the impact of each stair against his ribs as he went sliding down, catching up with the machine-gun at the bottom and rolling over on his back.

The little killer was slow, McGraw could hear his hefty footfalls as he rushed down the stairs for him. *"I'LL KILL YA! I'LL KILL YA!"*

He heaved and spun the gun toward the bottom of the second-floor stair-set and pulled the trigger, spraying wildly about the area where he thought he'd heard the movement. He dipped the gun up and down, left and right. He kept unloading. Sawdust came powdering down onto him along with giant splinters of oak, cutting his face and blurring his vision. But he kept shooting. He kept the bombardment up until the only thing coming from the muzzle of the gun was smoke.

A weight came crashing down where he'd been shooting, finally slamming onto the same landing he had, along with a blunt plopping. Using the Tommy gun as a prop, he worked himself back up the stairs, and could see the tiny hand in a black sleeve laying still by a snub-nose revolver. He made it to the top of the stairs, but before he could reach for the gun he heard a pistol cock from above.

He looked up to see Reed. Lip split, but gun steady. Using the guard-rail as a support.

The former partners eyed each other down coldly. McGraw spoke first. "Looks like you've gotta do this one on your own, Mike."

"You asshole! What the hell was your problem anyway? Why did you go out of your way to blow this thing up?"

"Is that how you see it?" McGraw asked.

"You're a hypocrite, George. You killed Benny Stanton. Shot him down like a mad mongrel. Admitted so to me and Undger just today! *How the hell is this any different? Tell me that!"*

"The girl, Mike."

"What?" he asked nonplussed. What *girl?*"

"Exactly Mike. You don't even remember her. Sure, I killed Stanton. But I walked up close and did it myself. And I didn't get some psychopathic hitmen to rack-up the collateral damage by killing a waitress and some ex-con."

"*An accident!* An accident, George! It happens every day, all the time. But everything that's happened since has been on you George! What happens now is on *you.*"

"Be sure to chisel that on my stone."

Reed smirked and shook his head disapprovingly. "Jesus, George." He rose his revolver and straightened his arm then. McGraw knew he was dead. He couldn't duck it. If he dove anywhere but back down the stairs he'd get unloaded on in a corner, and if he didn't break his neck pulling that stunt again, he still wouldn't have a gun to fight with. "You always were a hard-headed bastard."

There was a sudden bloody explosion just below Reed's chest, the gun flipped out of his hands and fell below, he spread his arms as though he were going to fly. And then he went crashing through the guard-rail and down onto the bottom set of stairs in front of McGraw.

From the spiked mouth of the second-floor railing, Charlie Giante stood with Undger's automatic in his hands. He let the gun slid from his grip and said nothing. Only sat at the top of the stairs and looked on introspectively at the carnage.

A pained groan came from below.

McGraw limped halfway down the stairs to his dying former partner. He bent on his good leg and rolled Reed over. The detective opened his eyes and started laughing, his teeth coated in blood, stopping for brief breaths when the pain was too much, but starting up again each time.

McGraw took a seat beside him and shook a cigarette loose and offered it in Reed's direction. The detective laughed a bit louder; groaned louder too. "You're gonna let me have this one, right?"

McGraw took the cigarettes and held one close enough for Reed to bite onto. Then struck a match with his thumb and lit them both. When Reed exhaled he coughed, and bits of blood spotted what little white was left of his shirt. But still, he laughed. "Guess the wives'll be pretty sore. No insurance for 'em, no more alimony checks. Good."

Smoke poured from McGraw's nostrils as he studied his own wound. "There any point in keeping that kid up there under guard to testify?"

Reed coughed out more blood. "No."

"Nobody left?"

"Nobody."

McGraw took another long draw from his smoke and asked, "That true, about O'Neil and Frost?"

Reed shut his eyes, ground his teeth, and nodded.

McGraw only shook his head and kept smoking.

A minute or so passed, the only sound coming from Reed writhing in agony. Then he mumbled, "So it was the girl from the liquor store that got you going on this? You? Six-Shot McGraw?"

"I guess I'm just the sentimental-type beneath it all."

"Nah ... you always were a hard-headed bastard..." Reed's words trailed off, and his eyes leered into eternity.

McGraw didn't get up; he didn't need or want to. He had at least one bullet in his leg, and besides, lead didn't get thrown around in the city like that without somebody calling the law. He guessed the manager had done so when he first blew out Undger's kneecap.

And so, he sat there; halfway up the first set of stairs, bleeding, smoking, waiting. Just him, the last witness, and the dead.

II

IT Comes in Threes

Richard could see her. She was driving the Mercedes, merging into the carpool lane of the terminal. The windows were dark. Too dark. "Tinted" is what they call them when they're that dark. He didn't like them, but they'd been her idea, and he'd never been able to say "No" to her. Ever. She wasn't the kind of woman you said "No" to. Through the shaded glass, he could see that abundance of garnet-hair he'd loved for so many years. When the sedan came closer he could even see the rubies dangling from each of her lobes; earrings he'd given her just last year as an anniversary gift. They were perfect for her. Even now. He thought they might look pretentious on other women; like they might be attempting to project an image of Romanian royalty. But never on her.

His stomach churned, but he'd already chewed up his last roll of Tums.

She parked beside him and emerged from the car. She was smiling. She looked just as he'd imagined she would. Red feathered-hair, her buxom features obvious even under that fur-coat. Her heels rapping against the concrete as she trudged the short distance around the grill to him.

He embraced her hug. Inside, a cruel, intangible hand tightened its grasp, twisting his intestines like a carny might a thin-balloon. "Hello, Rita," he breathed into her ear.

"I've missed you so, dear. Happy Birthday!"

He held her tighter.

"How was your flight?"

"Uneventful. But I thought of you the entire time."

This seemed to please her, and she tugged him by the jacket to the car. He tipped the skycap and shrugged it off when the young man pointed out that he'd handed him a twenty. Richard climbed behind the

59

wheel and when the boy was finished loading his bags he waved them off.

"I've made our reservation at Brannigan's and reserved our table. And Sean is going to meet us at The Pierre tonight. I tried to keep you to myself, but it seems everyone just *had* to see the birthday boy. But I'll get you alone later."

She kept her hand on his leg the entire drive to Brannigan's. When they arrived a pretty, young hostess showed them to their usual booth at the window. He enjoyed watching the sea. In all the years they'd been dining there, Richard spent most of his meals taking in the ocean-line and the docked fishing boats where the gulls constantly perched, providing only the dutiful grunts of awareness as his beautiful wife carried on one-way conversations.

Tonight, she had all his attention. Rita told him all about her doleful weekend; of the lonesome idle hours, spent rereading the last erotic paperback she'd snagged from the bestsellers rack, and having her hair colored a month early to spend an afternoon in the rush-hour of salon gossip. But mostly just missing him. Waiting for him to come back.

He knew she was lying.

He ordered the Salisbury steak, extra potatoes and onions, along with a Molson. Rita had the salad. She always had the salad. Of course she did, she had that enticing figure to worry about; the same maintained shape that had won him over so many years ago. He'd wondered in the last few days, on top of everything else, if he'd still love her if she were to become fat. Or even too gauntly. He thought, yes, he would.

He would always love her. She would always be his.

Richard took the final bite of his steak, and almost as though they'd been lying in wait, a group of waiters appeared and broke into a painful falsetto: "Happy Birthday to you! Happy Birthday to you!"

He smiled at her the entire time. When the waiters finished they left a small chocolate cake with a scoop of melting vanilla ice cream behind, a single candle burning in its center. He wondered at what point they stopped using the exact number of candles for the recipient's age.

He cut pieces for the two of them. She ate hers, but he could only glare down at his.

"Excuse me, dear. I won't be a minute." He wiped his mouth and rose from the table.

"Hurry back, Richard. I'd hate to eat all your birthday cake."

He sauntered to the back of the restaurant and into a dim corridor, past a short fellow who turned out to be the only one in the men's room. He was glad. Richard stared into the same mirror he must have used countless times before and smiled at himself. He couldn't hold it anymore. He turned around and lunged for a stall, retching into the bowl. Once more, and then he gagged on his own sickness for about a minute. He kicked the stall-door shut and sat-up against the wall. He flushed the commode and listened out for any others coming in as his thirty-five-dollar dinner literally went down the drain. "Pull it together, man. Pull it together."

Disgusted by his own nerves, he spat the thick, acrid taste into the bowl. Why should he be so shaken? It was going the way he'd thought it would. She hadn't seen him coming out of the cab fifteen minutes ahead of her at the airport. She didn't know that he'd been back since the day before. She hadn't seen him. He'd seen her. Watched her as she went to *his* apartment; she'd been carrying champagne with her the last time, as though that final night of his supposed absence had been something to celebrate. But that hadn't been when he decided to kill her. He'd decided to kill her back home, in Little Rock. That last day before leaving when he hadn't caught any fish. He'd caught three the day before. He thought about the three that entire last day; maybe that was why he hadn't caught any others.

His legs were still trembling as he pulled himself up. He knew he needed to do it soon or it would never be done at all. The gun was in his bag. A .38 he'd picked up in a sporting goods store back home. The portly hillbilly who'd sold it to him had kept insisting on the magnums. Richard declined each time, unable to explain how he didn't want something that would completely annihilate his beautiful wife's face. He couldn't tell the man that though she'd betrayed him in the worst way possible, he wanted her punishment to be instantaneous; without pain. Not too much fear. He wanted her to know he loved her, but that he was disappointed by her, and that he would be in so much more pain about it than she would be. And then it would be over.

But he had to do it now.

~ ~ ~

After paying the check they climbed into the Mercedes and Richard pulled onto the highway and started uptown.

"You just missed our exit, dear," Rita said.

"I've got my own little surprise. I thought we'd go somewhere. Just for a bit."

"I thought you wanted to meet Sean for drinks?"

"I do. And I will. It's early, he'll be there forty minutes from now. Come on … you can't refuse the birthday boy."

"Oh Richard, you're trouble."

A few miles down he took an exit to a town called Julton. If it meant anything to Rita yet, she didn't let on. Richard pulled into the first service station he saw. "Would you mind getting me some cigarettes, dear. My stomach is acting up."

"I wish you wouldn't smoke so much."

"Last pack. I promise."

He watched her strut into the store and then he slinked out of the car and popped the trunk. He'd forgotten the exact shirts he'd hidden the gun between and had an internal moment of panic when it wasn't under the first one. But he found it towards the bottom. He didn't look at it. He watched the station door as he dropped the revolver into his jacket. He climbed back into the car and flipped on the radio; somewhere in the Atlantic a hurricane was forming and meant trouble for Florida, and the shrill, overly-enthused voice of the stations commercial speaker promised an upcoming round of the most influential love songs from the Home of The Golden Oldies.

Now, he thought. If it's not now, it'll just go on. And that would be worse than anything. It can't go on, not with *him*. Maybe it could've been anyone but him: Ed, the lanky four-eyed numbers man from the office he brought around the house for poker nights. That would certainly be humiliating, but it would be different than her being with *him*. Or maybe even with Zach; the self-proclaimed ladies' man who seemed to have made it his mission in life to let his buddies know he could have any woman he wanted if he felt like it. Maybe. But it wasn't.

A minute later, Rita came back out with his cigarettes and they drove deeper into Julton.

~ ~ ~

He only found the dirt road because the ramshackle remains of the old house still stood at the end of the long, vacant highway, watching over what had been regarded as Lovers' Lane for anyone who could find their way there and got a kick out of the ghost stories surrounding the place. There was supposed to have been an old couple that lived in that house up until the twenties. The story was, their son enlisted in the first World War and came back cold, bitter, and missing half of his face. Some people said the gas the Germans used made him crazy. They said there used to be neighbors (though no one knew where they were supposed to have lived, as there was only one house around) that would see the disfigured veteran roaming aimlessly up and down the lane as though he were waiting for something to come along. One night, no one exactly knew when, the man killed the couple with his trench knife and then went down the dirt road by the house and cut his own throat. His specter supposedly haunted the place; murdering any lustful teenagers unlucky enough to screw around on his land. Richard and Rita had been there every other day for months at a time when they were first dating. Before either had their own place out of the dorms, or had even considered moving in together. They never saw anything supernatural on that road, but the excitement was there each time. A sense of isolation. Of danger.

She recognized the macabre scene of their early romance and was delighted.

As he pulled onto the road, her hand was back on his leg, inching its way to his inner thigh. She was almost touching the gun in his pocket.

When they were down the road and the mouth of sky disappeared from where they'd come from, Richard parked the car.

It was quiet, aside from the radio. And dark. The headlights offered the only light, other than the ghostly eye of a great white ball peering down at them from the sky like a steady, omnipotent spotlight. Waiting. Expecting. Urging.

"Richard..."

From the radio, mellifluous words of love and wisdom sounded out from The King: "...wise men say...only fools rush in..."

The sickness inside of him seethed. His hands numbed the way they did when he vomited. The worse he felt, the louder the music seemed to become.

"...but I can't help, falling in love ... with ... you..."

"Richard, I really have missed you. I know those fishing trips back where you grew-up are good for you, but these last few days I've just really wanted you back here with me."

If it had been anybody else. Ed, Zach, the cable guy, the fucking maid, Jesus. But not him. Not his best friend. Not the sensitive, successful artist who'd been with them since college. The only one who'd been with them from the beginning. The two humans he trusted implicitly. It was unforgivable. It was so serious that in the beginning he'd denied it. Smiled and drank away the pain, silently. But after that was over, he followed her. It was true; every time she went out she went to *his* apartment. And she'd always lie about where'd she'd been. Every time, so easily. He'd almost hired a Private Detective to follow the both of them, but what would have been the point in that? He'd caught them. He didn't want anyone else to know how'd they hurt him. It had been going on for a least a month. He watched *him* greet her at the door once, but that was the most he saw. He didn't want to see anything else. He imagined them in that apartment – he'd been in it many times himself. He wondered if *he* fucked her in his studio on top of a blank canvas, their nude bodies drenched in paint, laughing at him; snickering, lecherous fiends indulging in a loving husbands'

ignorance. On the other side of his best friends'
apartment door Richard imagined loathsome acts of
perversion carried out in a deliberate means to shame
him. Every time she kissed him he thought the worst
and had to brush his teeth.

"Richard? Richard, what did you have in mind?"

If it had been anyone else.

He thought about the steelhead he'd pulled out of
the river that first day in Little Rock; the three of them.
Lifeless, ugly, alien corpses that had been deceived
with a hook, and caught with the same. There were
three of them: Sean, Rita, and Richard.

The best friend, the wife, and the cuckold.

"Listen Richard, we'd better start out soon. Sean is
certain to be at The Pierre by now."

Her saying *his* name did it. She'd said it earlier in
the night, maybe more than once even. But never while
he'd been thinking of them ... together.

He jerked for the gun. He'd planned on telling her
that he knew, and that he loved her, but didn't forgive
her. He'd planned on slipping the short muzzle of the
revolver around the back of her seat and in between the
head cushion. He'd planned on her not having to see it
coming. But when she said *his* name then, he exploded.
"Sean is certain to be *in the fucking ground tonight!*"

Rita watched her husband take the gun out; the
hammer only briefly snagging, ripping strings out in
the fabric of his jacket. And then suddenly it was in her
face. *"Richard!"* He pulled the trigger and watched the
hammer rise and fall just before he shut his eyes. *Click.*
He opened them; Ritas' own were crossed, staring into
the black-eye of the .38 in her face. He pulled the
trigger again and she flinched. *Click. Click, click, click.*
Each time the hammer dropped and the cylinder spun,
each time Rita jumped and blinked in rapid

successions, never taking her eyes off the guns' barrel. Each time it dry-fired.

And Richard remembered the box of shells he'd hidden inside a pair of dress socks. They were still in his bag. He never even loaded the goddamn thing.

He took the gun away from her, gawking at it as though it had betrayed him. Rita's jaw bounced up and down like a ventriloquists' stuttering dummy.

He knew it was too late. He dropped the gun and pounced on her before she could speak. He didn't want her to talk to him. Snarling and cursing, he wrapped his hands around her neck. He was strangling her, and just before her tongue jutted from her mouth for good she managed to croak: "Ri ... why..."

"*Because I love you too much!*" he screamed in her face.

Her eyes bulged in their sockets, her hands clasped onto his as they choked her, her feet put up the most struggle behind him until one finally stilled against the dash; her heel had caught on the volume knob and was cranking the music up and down. "...Ri..."

"...like a river flows, surely to the sea, darling so it goes, some things are meant to be..."

"Because I love you too much. And *he* can't have you!"

Her hold on his hands weakened. And finally, her foot dropped to the console, spinning the volume all the way. And he knew she was dead. Not so much because her body went limp, but because he'd watched something go out of her eyes. She didn't look afraid anymore.

"...take my hand ... take my whole life too..."

He opened the door and fell out of the car. The love song went resounding into the night, and his dead, slumped-up wife watched him crawl in the dirt, crying, gagging. He wanted to let the sickness out of him but there was nothing left. And so he gagged.

"...for I can't help falling in love with you..."

Still on his knees, he lifted himself. Gawking into the cold light of the moon hanging above him, still, watching. Showing no gratification. Only knowing that there was more, telling him he wasn't finished. That if he could do that, he could do anything.

"I know. I know."

There was more, but the worst part was behind him.

He spoke to the sky, "I haven't forgotten about you Sean."

~ ~ ~

Sean was waiting at the bar when Richard arrived at The Pierre. The artist stood out amongst the slew of stock-brokers and lawyers. Instead of a double-breasted suit with cuff links he donned a leather coat and a pair of black Brutinis. Rockstar-length hair curling just above his shoulders was another crowd-only. Sean had often told him that he'd spent most of his teenage summers with his mother in Hell's Kitchen; a part-time slum kid, who'd taken his daddy's offer to pay for his schooling, only to drop out half way through after impressing a gallery owner who knew all the right people. He'd long since been bumping shoulders with the best of them, and still he dressed like that. Maybe that rugged individualism had been what lured Rita to him. Or maybe the way he never seemed to have a thinner or thicker shadow of bristle on his face had been what won her over.

He'd shoot him through that face.

He spotted Richard from the bar and raised his glass; no doubt a soda-pop. As a successful artist, Sean was obliged to a life-long substance abuse problem he could conveniently fly off the rails of.

"Richard, you old-dog, you already losing track of the hours? If this were whiskey I'd have drowned by now."

Richard sneered and patted him on the shoulder. "Whiskey Sour," he told the bartender. The gun in his pocket clanked against the bar as he took his stool, but no one seemed to notice. He'd been sure to load all five chambers this time.

"Get the birthday boy a double, on me," said Sean. "So, how was the motherland? Catch anything decent?"

"I wouldn't say decent," Richard spoke into his drink. The liquor burned going down, at first frothing bursting bubbles of pain in his stomach, and then all at once numbing him completely.

"Where's Rita? I thought she'd be here tonight? As a matter of fact, she told me she would."

"She wasn't feeling well. I dropped her off at home."

"Really? She said that?"

How dare he. "You two talk a lot while I was gone?" It came out before he could think better.

Sean looked to him like he'd been lightly slapped. And then he grinned. "You've always been a funny guy, Dick. This time it wasn't so funny."

"I guess I didn't realize I was trying to be."

"You're serious?"

Richard took a drink.

"So, what, one of the three amigos ain't allowed to speak to the other now? That it?"

Richard still didn't answer him.

"You're a funny guy, Dick," he tossed a bill on the bar and stood.

"Hold on, Sean." He stopped him before he could walk off. "I'm just tired. I ... I didn't mean anything."

Sean didn't speak. But he didn't leave.

"Come on. Sit down, let's have a good time."

Sean moved back by his stool. "Rita really said she was sick? I talked to her just a couple hours ago about you two meeting me here. You obviously got the message."

He wanted to yank out the .38 and plug him right there. Questioning his word about the whereabouts of *his* wife. As though that were any sort of rightful business of his. "Tell you what ... how about we go to my place. We'll have a drink ... or a soda ... and you can see her for yourself."

"Well actually," Sean said, "I've got something I want to show you. I guess it's kind of a surprise."

Richard's face tightened. "Here?"

"Yea, that's right."

"You've got a surprise ... for me..."

"Don't look so forlorn, Oldman. I think you're going to like it."

"A surprise."

"Now he's catchin' on." Sean stood and gestured for Richard to follow.

What could he say? No Sean, *you* follow *me* because I've got my own little surprise. That's right, just over here into the parking lot; that's where he thought he'd do it. Pop the trunk and allow the ghastly, transfixing sight of Rita's corpse to prod him with a harsh surge of reality just before he blew his head off. He'd topple over into the trunk, Richard would shut it, and then he'd be on his way.

Only now he was taking *him* somewhere. He followed Sean to the hotel elevators, the shaded-glow of the lobby lights gave the sandy-marble walls of the vestibule a haunted, almost orange tinge. They loaded into the car with a group of others, the young operator never took his eyes away from the panel of buttons. Richard stood in the corner, his hands in his jacket pockets. They got off on the fortieth-floor and the blood began pounding in Richards ears, he knew where Sean was taking him, and he hated him for it. He was taking him to the same suite that he'd proposed to Rita in right after graduation. Sean had been there. It had been a place of ceremonial significance between the three of them; he and Rita because of their engagement, and Sean simply because he'd been their closest friend; the best man. He'd been the one to pop the first cork when she said yes, showering them both in Dom Perignon.

And now he was taking him there. Richard couldn't understand why. And then it occurred to him that this could be it; Sean's stand. Maybe Rita *was* supposed to be here tonight. Maybe they were going to stand up to him. Say, this is it, Dick, old boy. We're leaving you. We thought it only right to end it where it began in a sense.

As they moved down the corridor Sean was carrying on about the after-party of his first art show; he was going on about the old days. Richard wasn't listening. Richard could only think about how he couldn't wait to kill Sean; actually *couldn't* wait. He'd kill him in that room. Soon as he opened that door. It couldn't wait for outside, it had to end here. He'd let off a single shot, Sean would fall to the floor, and then he'd shut the door and walk off. Maybe he'd make it to the elevator and down to the lobby, maybe he wouldn't. Right now, that didn't matter. All that mattered was that Sean died.

They were there. In front of the door. Sean fished for his key and grinned at Richard. "Close your eyes."

"What?"

"I promised someone I'd make you close your eyes."

"Oh."

"Now keep them closed until I tell you."

He never shut his eyes, and when Sean turned around and unlocked the door Richard pulled out the revolver. It snagged quietly (much the way it had earlier) in his pocket and then it's short barrel was pushing against the back of Sean's head. He jerked the trigger as the door opened; the blast was louder than he could've imagined, a bullet went ripping through the back of Sean's skull and exploded out of his forehead and into the ceiling.

"*Happy Birthday!*" the room of guests sang out as they were stippled in Sean's blood. And then they were screaming. Sean crumpled to the floor and Richard could see them. All of them. It was a surprise party alright.

There was: Ed and Zach, they were up front with Richards' young secretary, Mary Ann; and then there was Stan and Jill Penzler, the older couple from the apartment next door; Richards Director from the office, Mike Sultan; there were nearly a dozen others, co-workers, neighbors, plenty of friendly-faces that were now contorted in an ugly blend of horror and incredulity.

Richard was aware of his friends, crying and brushing past him – mindful of the blood pooling around the sprawled-out figure by the door. But he wasn't looking at them, he was looking at Rita. There, in the center of the room, displayed proudly in the middle of where the crowd had been gathered, she looked to him; her brilliant blue eyes a soft-pastel, no larger than the size of quarters. She looked to him with all the love and vivaciousness she'd demonstrated throughout their marriage. There was no hate and no fear in her eyes. She watched him from an ornate-honey frame, her face flecked in spots of blood like ominous crimson freckles.

The world seemed to stir; lucidity surfing the dizzy-waves of a brooding sea just ahead of a storm of devastating comprehension. Richard's skull felt more like a shaken soda-can. And the sickness had never been worse.

For over a decade – long before the troubles – Richard had pleaded with Sean to paint Ritas' portrait. It had begun as a breeze-shooter, but gradually transformed into an obsession. Sean had always refused, telling him that if what he created did not live up to the expectations of a naturalistic, mirror image of her, he'd never forgive him. Richard had always assured him that this wouldn't be so, but Sean still wouldn't hear of it. This kept up for years until Richard had given up altogether on pressuring Sean to do the deed. But he never let him forget about it.

Or Rita. Rita had known. He'd often brought it up in front of the two, in the hopes it would incite Sean into going through with it.

He finally had. And Richard couldn't help but admire the work of his two closest friends.

Other pictures began to take shape; one-by-one, like stark puzzle pieces in Richard's reeling mind. Simple things, like: why Rita might've been spending all that time in Sean's apartment (where he happened to work) and why she would lie about it. Why Sean had stopped inviting him over. Why she'd never seemed to spend the night there, even that last night, when she thought he was out of town... with the champagne ... maybe they'd been celebrating the completion of something after all.

Simple things. The driving forces of murder.

Richard moved deeper into the room; mindful of his best friend's body, but not bothering to avoid the pool of blood. He looked down at the artist, the only sensation even remotely relatable to relief was that Sean hadn't seen it coming. But Rita *had*. Rita had suffered at *his* hands. He thought of her in the trunk of that car down in the parking garage as his shoes squished lightly along the carpet, a red-trail of footprints followed him to the bar by the window. He poured himself a bourbon, not troubling with ice cubes or a water chaser, listening to the formidable reverberations of sirens belting along somewhere down below. He knew it was too soon, but he couldn't help but feel that they were coming for him. He gulped down the last of his drink and sauntered back over to the middle of the room and stood in front of her. He felt like she had the right to watch. He shut his eyes, the steel of the muzzle was cold beneath his chin. A minute later he opened them to hers and pulled the trigger.

III

A Killer Scoop

One

"**T**ASK FORCE ASSEMBLED IN GROWING MANHUNT FOR PSYCHO KILLER

"**Switchblade Slayer Still At Large; Likely Out of City, Police Say**

"**By Fred Conte**

"Over the past six months the working-class neighborhood of Dunbar has been plagued by the most deplorable sort of being mankind has to offer, as a murderer, known only as the "Switchblade Slayer", has been using its shadowed streets and unwary occupants for his own depraved minds sinister desires. The killer's name obviously derives from his weapon of choice: a stiletto switchblade knife.

"Three women: 27-year old Kathern Stark, 21-year old Mary Stuart, and 36-year old Elizabeth Greer have all met brutal ends within a block of their own residences. Police admit that from the start, it was clear the killings were connected, and each committed by the same perpetrator.

"It was also thought that each attack was planned meticulously, after the killer familiarized himself with the victim's daily routine and knew when each would be most vulnerable; however, Lieutenant Brody, veteran detective and lead investigator in the Slayer case, has been most candid with the press in his latest interview and has openly stated that this theory has changed, and that it is now widely believed the killer is nothing more than a deranged opportunist, seeing young, attractive women on the city streets and striking when their backs were turned.

"Lt. Brody has also shared some of the killer's features, theorized and provided by a reputable criminal profiler: the murderer is thought to be a diminutive, middle-aged male, extremely reticent and anti-social in nature. He likely has a low IQ, and quite possibly, even a mental defect.

"Lt. Brody stated that it was more vital than ever to share this information with the public, as it is now speculated that the killer has fled the city. The Lt. wouldn't go into detail as to how this information came about, but he did confirm that a specially selected group of trained officers have been assembled in a search that will now reach across state lines.

"The Lieutenant went on to say that no matter how far this maniac may have gotten, it's only a matter of time before he's apprehended, and held in front of the courts to face the harshest penalty for his crimes.

~ ~ ~

"The switchblade knife used in the killings..."

"Will you *please* stop reading that *grisly* material out loud," said the blue hair in the fur-coat sitting to the right of the woman who'd been reading the article. "So, *morbid*."

"Horrendous," said the one on the left. "To think there was someone like that in this very neighborhood. A madman! Walking the same streets, sharing the same taxis, shopping in the same delicatessens!"

From the middle: "Well he's gone now, Minnie. And good-riddance! There are enough switchblade wielding hoodlums running around this neighborhood; with those leather jackets, and *tattoos*..."

From the right: "I still say it's nothing to be discussed in public.

"Excuse me! More coffee, miss."

The waitress moseyed over, filled the woman's cup, waited for a thank you that never came, and then

78

drifted back to the other end of the counter. Halfway down she got a que from the man who'd been slouched over every cup of coffee he'd ordered for the last hour. He was drunk; that twistin' the night away without any music, drunk. He wasn't bad though, worse had come in. Her only complaint was that he spoke a little loudly, as if he knew his diction would be slurred and was therefore overcompensating for it. And his eyes were so narrow, it looked more like he was shouting in his sleep whenever he thanked her. This time he only grunted something inaudible, and she went on to her spot by the register.

She took advantage of the moment and lit a cigarette. Inhaling the smoke deeply, it gave her the first soothing sensation she'd felt since before the dinner-crowd. Her feet hurt from standing all day, and there was a hole in the toe of one of her stockings that caused the bare skin to rub against the inside of her heel. At least it's late, she thought. In about an hour she'd clean up as the last of the customers finished and left, then she'd lock up, go home, and sleep for a whole four hours before waking up to start all over again.

Her name was Joanna, but she *hated* being called that; so, to the world it was Joan Fuller. She was short, slender, with dark-hair and doe eyes that pleaded for respect; though they meant to demand it. And this wasn't the first time she'd used her moments of leisure to fill her head with thoughts of daily monotony and pessimistic musing over her personal life and unfulfilled professional aspirations: just things like the fact that she was thirty-two and single. Never married, never even proposed to. And not a single thing to indicate that she'd be out of the diner anytime soon.

She'd wanted to be an actress once. Like most young women with this desire, she'd come to the city to make it big. But just like most of these women, nothing came of it. She was pretty enough, sure, but so were a few hundred other women; women still in their early twenties. The auditions had stopped nearly four years ago, and the odd jobs had piled on. The city had worn on her since, losing its anything-is-possible nostalgia and vibrancy it had been so alive with when she'd first come by bus. Lately, she'd entertained the notion of leaving the city; not for home, she didn't have it in her to go back there and go through everyone she'd known picking her apart when they asked what happened and she admitted defeat. But somewhere back down South. Somewhere quiet.

This was what she was thinking about while glaring off into a corner of the room, unconsciously moving to ash her cigarette, and instead knocking over the coffee pot and sending a flood of black, sweet-smelling drink all over the steak and potatoes of the man sitting at the edge of the counter.

"*Oh, my gosh!* I'm so sorry, I didn't even see..."

She wiped at the counter and around the irreparably soggy plate of food, as the man rose from his stool; he didn't look angry with her, in fact, he seemed as innocently embarrassed by the spill as she was. He grabbed a napkin and helped stop the overflow on his side of the counter. "That's ok, miss. Really. Just one of those things bound to happen."

"I'm just glad my boss didn't see that," she said, trying to joke away the flush of abashment she felt rising in her face.

"Well, we'll just make it our little secret," he said.

She tossed the wet rag and went to start another pot. When she turned back, she could see he was still smiling at her, but now his eyes were riding the unblinking-line between amiable and flirtatious. He was tall, clean-shaven, with dark-hair she could just make out under the brim of his hat. And eyes that were kind, but with cloudy, enigmatic features. She thought he was handsome enough, but above all he was familiar.

After the older women who'd been reading the paper paid and left – and after the pudgy drunk motioned for a refill, before looking into his cup and seeing it was still full, then laughing it off – Joan went back to the other end of the counter.

He smiled as she approached.

"Our cook, Robby, is about to take off but I could tell him to whip-up one more steak if you'd like; on the house, of course."

"Don't bother, I wasn't really hungry. I was tired of looking at it anyway, you did me a favor."

She tittered politely and suddenly she knew why he was familiar. "I've seen you in here before, haven't I?"

"Well yes, I suppose you have."

"Do you live in the neighborhood?"

His smile partially waned. "No. Not exactly. I do a lot of business around here, so to say."

She leaned closer. "So, what's the big mystery?"

"Mystery?"

"Yea, this business of yours. What keeps you in this neck of the woods?"

He grinned and hunched a little closer. "No mystery. See, I'm a detective."

She stood erect. "A detective? No kidding." She eyed him over. "Not coming here on business, are you?"

He laughed light-heartedly and shook his head. "No, no. I've been on patrol in the neighborhood the last few weeks. Until today that is. This just kind of became my favorite place to come and ... take a break," he finished with a smile.

She'd taken his hint (one learns all the hints when they experience them almost every day) and gave a polite grin, but was more interested in what he'd said before that. "And what happened today?"

"Oh, they just don't need my type around here anymore. Place is safe, now anyway.

"Don't suppose you've been reading the paper?"

"Sure I have," she said.

"Then you already know all about it."

She was puzzled momentarily, but thought of what the older woman who'd been reading the paper had said. "You don't mean ... you're talking about that killer, aren't you?"

He nodded.

"They say he skipped town. Anything to it?"

"Sure there is," he assured her. "And that's exactly why it's my last night in Dunbar."

"Last one, huh? Well we'll be sorry to lose your business."

"Well, how about making a night of it? I know a good late-night show."

"That's awful nice of you to ask, but I think I just want to go straight to sleep when I get off here," she said with a little extra teeth to the otherwise routinely anodyne rejection.

He gave an easygoing shrug to match the grin. "Suit yourself. Can't blame a guy for trying though." He stood and put down several bills; leaving her a tip larger than the cost of the meal. "Just the same, it was nice to finally speak to you, miss..."

"Joan. Joan Fuller." She held her hand out and instead of shaking it, he took hold of her gently by the fingers; his thumb lightly caressed the knuckles from her index to her pinky.

The way he was holding her hand, she was sure he'd try and kiss it; like all the egghead high society types from the romance films. But he didn't. "I'm Michael. Michael Brown."

"Well thanks again, Michael. And thanks for keeping the neighborhood safe."

He tipped his hat, and just when she thought he was turning to go, he didn't. He smiled at her a second longer, then said: "Goodnight, Joan." Then he turned around and sauntered out the door – coincidentally the same time the drunkard slapped a five down and stumbled his own way to the exit, and when he made it, Brown was there to hold the door for him. The slurring man began launching a volley of gratitude as the door eased shut and cut off the outside world.

And Joan was glad; though the detective was physically attractive, some people are just too forward with their intentions, even when it's clear they're trying not to be. It was still sort of nice; being flirted with by someone who wasn't old enough to be her father.

Things can always get better.

Across the room, a man with his wife signaled for two more coffees.

Two

She was clearing the couples table when he came in. When she heard the door open she was sure it was going to be the detective, back for a second try; but it wasn't. The man who'd come into the diner, less than fifteen minutes before she was going to close, was a complete stranger. She was sure he'd never come in before; though she couldn't remember every face that came in and out of the place, she was positive she'd have remembered his. His face was sharp and narrow and there was something about his eyes that she could see even from across the room; the skin under those eyes were the kind of drooping dark that came from a condition Joan referred to as, perpetual exhaustion; a condition brought on by working every day of your life and seemingly getting nowhere from it. This might've been presumptuous of her, it was just that that look of depleted vigor was more familiar than any diner patron could ever be.

The stranger seemed to notice Joan, too. But those firm, weary eyes took him to the jukebox setup by the door; he fed the machine, and the mellifluous lyrics that played out sent an electric wave of incredulity through her:

"...you give your hand to me, and then you say hello... and I can hardly speak ... my heart is beating so..."

It was Ray Charles' "You Don't Know Me." Her favorite song. No one had touched that box all night, and here comes this stranger and the first thing he does is play *that* song.

"...and anyone can tell ... you think you know me well ... but you don't know me..."

He sat almost exactly where the detective had earlier, and she went to him. She knew she should say that the place would not only be closed in a few minutes, but that the cook had already taken off. But what came out was: "I love this song."

He smiled at her.

"Do you want some coffee?"

He didn't answer. He was still locked in that close-up look in her eyes. "Do you really like this song?" he asked.

"I ought to, I listen to it enough. I've got that very record at the front of my collection."

That grin widened and she could see he had all his teeth, "What's your name?"

"Joanna," she said without thinking. "Don't call me that though. Just Joan."

"Well I think I like this song, too, Just Joan."

She laughed without meaning to. "And what's yours?"

He looked down in his hands and rubbed at his palms, as though massaging a callous. "Call me, John."

"And what is it you do, Call Me John?"

It was like he was talking to his hands, "Oh, I'm a working man." That was when he looked back at her. "You know how it goes, just trying to get by."

Joan glared off to the jukebox as the song came to an end. "Yea. I know how it goes." She looked back to the stranger who was calling himself, John. "Can I ask you something kind of personal, John? What would you be. I mean... you know... if you could be anything?"

He cocked his head at a slight angle, like the question amused him. "Oh... I suppose I wanted to be a novelist, once upon a time. Nothing truly exotic."

"Wanted to be like Hemingway, huh?"

"Oh no," he said, but with no resentment. "Every writer has something different to say; It's as much about the delivery as it is the plot, and the way I see it, everyone has their own way of sharing a story. You can write about anything you want if you can make it into an experience. When I was a kid, growing up in Hells Kitchen, that old Underwood was the only thing that made me feel like I could be any different from the others. With it, I could be anyone I loved or anyone I hated; it was like I'd been gifted some tool that let me give an impression of how I saw the world..." He saw she was listening with sincere interest, but he felt he was rambling. "...but, things don't always work out. Bills have got to be paid; so, you start with something else, find out you're not half bad at it, and just kind of stick around ... I guess that's what I've been doing. Sticking around."

She didn't say anything. Except for his own occupation in the arts, the story sounded the same as hers. And though broken dreams weren't anything new, she found it extremely unusual that this man would admit that to her; some hash house honey he'd never met before.

He spoke again: "What about you, Just Joan? I can't imagine a woman like you dreamed of being a waitress her whole life."

She began to tell him. Then the pair on the other end of the diner paid and left. She took advantage of the moment and excused herself. As she cleared the table, she made a decision, and when she put the dishes away she went back to John and told him what he wanted to know.

And they talked.

Three

Ten minutes later Joan walked out of the diner; John held the door for her. They were the last two in the place, and Joan wouldn't have noticed the time if he had not asked her when her shift ended.

She took a set of keys from her bag, selected one, and engaged the lock of the door.

"Gee, I'm glad to be out of there."

"You don't like it much, do you?"

"What's to like?" she said. "Taking orders from a bunch of rude strangers all day. I'm sick of the smell of burgers and potatoes; the smell follows me everywhere."

"I know, it's making me hungry."

She laughed without meaning to. They were on the sidewalk now, and a silence had fallen between them. Even the nighttime background commotion of the city had tuned-out for the moment.

"Well ... goodnight..." she hadn't meant to say this, but that mounting surge of nerves had become overwhelming and she couldn't help herself.

"Do you live close?"

"Pretty close."

"Can I walk you home? The city is dangerous enough to walk through at night without some psychopath running around."

She looked sharply to him. "You mean the Slayer?"

The shade of his eyes abruptly changed and he gave an awkward impression of someone who'd said something he shouldn't have. They were ambling down the sidewalk now. "If that's what he's called."

"That's what todays paper's calling him," she said. "In a column written by the same guy who's been following the case. Don't you read the paper? It said he skipped town."

"Yea, well, sometimes they get it wrong," he said noncommittally.

"What do you mean?"

"Just that those newspapermen can write about whatever they want; whether it's to sell more copies, or their own *personal reasons* for spreading that garbage."

She stopped walking and looked to him. "Cynical, aren't we?"

"I try not to be," he took her gently by the arm and they were moving again. "You just shouldn't be putting yourself at risk based on what some gossip-pusher says."

"What am I supposed to do, blow my hard-earned pay on a cab ride to an apartment ten minutes away?"

"Like I said."

"Well I got it from more than just the paper you know. A detective came into the diner earlier tonight. He said they were on the level about the killer being out of Dunbar."

"A detective?"

"Yea, he comes in all the time, but I didn't know he was a detective until tonight."

"And this guy said the killer was out of the neighborhood?"

"Sure."

"What else did he say?"

"That was all. Like I said, I see him all the time, but tonight was the first time I ever said anything besides 'would you like a refill?'."

"Well, that's quite a scoop."

"I'll say."

"Did you like him?"

That got her tittering again. "Why, are you jealous?"

"Should I be?"

She smiled as they came to the end of a long brick building that was identical to every other on its street. "Well, this is me." She went up the first few stairs and met him at eyelevel. "Thanks for walking me home."

"Think nothing of it," he said. "Goodnight."

She knew it was her turn. "I don't think I have anything to drink ... but would you want some coffee? Upstairs I mean. In my apartment."

That crocodile grin spread, and he trotted up the stairs and held the door for her.

She led the way upstairs.

Four

"...No, you don't know the one
who dreams of you at night
and longs to kiss your lips
longs to hold you tight
Oh, I'm just a friend
that's all I've ever been
'cause you don't know me..."

The record spun and the soft, sweet-sounding melody played out as the two paced slowly in the middle of Joan's dimly lit living room. Her head just one or two tentative inches away from resting against his shoulder. She could feel his chin brush against the locks of her hair as they swayed steadily to the music. There was no real form or technique to their dance; they were simply holding one another.

She never started the coffee.

As the song ended and the next began, she glanced up to him, and that was when he tried to kiss her. She moved just enough that he kissed the edge of her mouth, where her lips ended and her cheek began, already hating herself for the instinctive brush-off. "I'm sorry."

"Don't be. Don't say a word.

"Well, maybe one..."

"What?"

"Can I use your washroom?"

She giggled and pointed down the hall. "On the left."

"Thanks," he said, taking his jacket off. He threw it onto the couch next to her coat. "Don't dance with anyone while I'm away." He went down the hall and she heard the door close.

She stood alone, smiling; her arms crossed and her palms gripping her shoulders. She went to the phonograph and flipped the record. As the other side began and she counted the seconds, she took both jackets from the couch and went to the rack by the door.

About halfway across the room was when the slip of paper fell from his jacket. She stopped. Thousands of possibilities rushed through her mind; most of them pessimistic. There's one way of knowing for sure, Joan thought: She could look.

She quickly resented herself for the thought, snatched the sheet up and continued to the rack. She hung her own coat, and then his. She meant to put the slip back in his pocket, she really did. But when she happened to notice the first word inside of the unfolding paper, she let herself read the second. And then the third. And then a few more.

The top read:
Fritz's Diner
MONDAY
Arrival: 7:30 am
Departure:

The sheet slipped from her fingers as she heard the bathroom door opening. It fluttered in between her feet as poisoned thoughts stirred like treacherous rapids through her mind; literally making her dizzy.

She'd never seen John before, that much she was certain of. Of course, he could've been in the diner on one of those rare occasions she was absent, but that paper had the schedule of someone's entire last week there... all the way to that afternoon.

The schedule couldn't be his own. Or if it was, then what was he doing there? And where was he during?

Waiting for John to come back into the room and then calmly inquiring as to the specifics of the sheet, *actually* occurred to her; there could be a completely innocent, and maybe even funny story to it, she thought.

But what she thought of immediately after was the way he'd been talking, back on the sidewalk; about the newspaper, and what he seemed to imply as false claims of a fleeing murderer. At first, she thought maybe he didn't care for the articles or maybe even had some sort of grudge against the author of them. But now she was thinking maybe he had another reason for such clear disdain of the column.

And why he'd suddenly seemed so curious and unsure when she'd mentioned the detective.

That did it; Joan was out of the apartment door and scurrying down the hall.

John came into the room then, just in time to catch the swinging door. He saw the open slip on the carpet.

"Joan!" he hollered and started after her, leaving the apartment door open and the music inside to spill out gently into the corridor.

She was just rounding the corner of the stairway as he ran down the hall, calling out: "*Joan!* Joan stop...."

There was more to it, but the words were muffled out by all the hurry and she didn't hear them; and she had no intention of letting him catch-up to make them clear. She dashed down one flight of stairs to another, until finally making it to the first floor. The echoing footfalls in the staircase continued and she knew it was him. "*Joan!*"

"Oh God, help!" she screamed, rushing down the hall for the buildings exit. "Somebody, please!"

Different faces appeared from odd doors as the terrified waitress kept on.

"Joan, stop!" he was at the bottom of the stairs now.

She didn't stop, and as she made it past the last apartments and to the exit doors, she looked back to see that two, older burley men had taken hold of John by each of his arms; he was writhing and kicking but getting nowhere from it. And he was still shouting to her, "Joan, Listen to me! Listen! You have to..."

But Joan was out of the doors and into the night.

Five

The streets of Dunbar were lonely. She wasn't sure how long she'd been walking, only that she couldn't remember a time the neighborhood had ever been so quiet; part of her was grateful for this. The sidewalks were hers, and hers alone.

She was still shaking. *How? How?* Joan thought. The question was, how could she have let herself be so stupid? She knew the answer. But how could someone like that, turn out to be so completely different.

She wondered if those men who'd been wrestling with John back at the apartments had been able to hold him; if the cops had shown up to arrest him. She supposed they wouldn't know *who* he was until she came forth. Maybe ... maybe they'd even let him go ... what did they really have to go on?

Maybe she should've stuck around.

No, she couldn't do that. She couldn't bear to look at *him* again.

But suppose they had let him go ... suppose he was out on the streets right now ... surely, he'd be looking for...

A dark sedan pulled to the curb beside her

The terror catapulted through her as a scream forced its way to audibility, then all at once was stifled as the figure stepped out of the car and revealed itself as Detective Michael Brown. "Hello Miss Fuller. Late night stroll?"

She broke down and sat on the curb, sobbing into her palms. The detective shut the car door and went to her. Bending down and taking hold of her shoulders, he said, "Now what could *you* possibly have to cry about?"

She told him; she told him all of it. And he was just as interested in this stranger, as the stranger had been in him.

"It was so awful when I found it ... I feel so stupid ... I invited him up myself!"

"Now just take it easy, it's all right now," he said reassuringly. "Now you say he had notes of *your* schedule at the diner?"

"It didn't say my name ... but who else could be there every day to keep track of? I'm in that hellhole more than the boss is!"

"But you don't have it?"

"Well, no ..."

"Did you read the times?"

"Times?"

"You said it was a record of when someone came and went. Did you check the times of each day?"

"Not really ... No. It all just happened so fast, I had to get out of there when I saw it. It all just made sense at once; the things he said and knew. God, he even knew the song I listen to the most!"

The detective grinned. She didn't say anything, but she couldn't believe he was grinning at a time like this. "No kidding? Well it's a good thing you got out of there when you did. Otherwise, I might not have found you out here.

"Come on, let's get out of the street."

He helped her up, and then opened the passengers' door for her. Then he got back behind the wheel and pulled away with Joan.

Six

THey pulled to the curb and Joan could see that they were next to the diner. "What're we doing here?" she found her voice was still stirred and quiet.

The detective killed the engine. "I've got to report this to the station. There's a phone, here, right?"

"Yes."

"And I just sort of figured you had a key to the place. You do have a key, don't you?"

"Yes."

"Well, then let's go."

They both got out of the car; this time he didn't open or close the door for her.

The night was still and the parking lot was barren. Suddenly it occurred to her she didn't have the key. It was back in her apartment. Back with him.

"Michael ... Michael I'm sorry. I left the key with my bag. I don't even have my coat. I don't have a way to get inside."

The features of his face changed to a hardened expression she took as the finality of his patience with her, but the detective smirked and thumbed his hat back at the brim. "Well, that's alright, Miss Fuller. A good policeman always has a way to get inside." He dug into his inner pocket and Joan realized for the first time that he was wearing gloves; she could hear the taut leather of them stretching as he produced a small black-case from inside his jacket. She'd half-expected a line of tailored cigarettes as he popped the case open, instead there was a group of tools, assorted side to side by size. The detective selected a long, thin instrument that Joan thought looked more like a metal toothpick. After that was a small, L-shaped piece. "Here we are now." He put the case away and moved to the door as Joan stepped aside. "Emergencies call, huh?" she realized he was speaking to her, but his back was turned and he was working at the lock. She sidled over and could see he had the sharp instrument in the bottom of the keyhole at an angle, cranking delicately up and down by the inch. The shorter part of the second tool was just above it, still, but at the same angle. Soon there was an audible click and the detective cranked the top piece to the right; there was a second click and he removed the tools quickly and pocketed them. "Nothing to it," he said absently.

The door opened and he held it ajar for her; offering her the lead into the darkness of that room ... where she'd met him. She looked back, even the street light had died. There was only darkness for Joan in either direction. She breathed heavy and stepped inside the dinner. Detective Michael Brown looked both ways into the night, saw nothing, and shut the door on it.

~ ~ ~

She flipped the switch and the fluorescents illuminated a room that somehow appeared long abandoned. Her visceral reaction was that she never wanted to see this place again. Its ugly tables and matching chairs set-up sporadically around the room without any delicacy or attractiveness in their placement. The paper-thin walls that typically passed along the blurred reverberations of the outside world. That damn 11x4 counter she spent most of her days behind, like a long, skinny one-man cell.

"The phones in the kitchen." She led the way and at first was sure he was following her, but once she made it past the archway and to the phone, she turned and didn't see him. "Michael?" Suddenly a shadow moved and the detective appeared in the doorway.

"Where'd you go?" He didn't say anything. He just stood there. Joan heard machinery click-clacking somewhere in the dinner. The sound – as clear and resound in the silence as if it were in the kitchen with them – was acutely familiar. "Michael?" His face was still a mask of icy indifference. "*Say something!*" And then she knew what that mechanical echo was coming from.

"...mmmmm, you don't love me ... mmmmm you don't know me..."

Her mouth gaped. "...I ... I ... the phones right here..." She spun around and took the phone from its cradle. A powerful hand came from behind and the device was out of her hands before she'd spun the dial. He hung it back on the wall. She began to back away, slowly. Cautiously. "What're you doing ... Michael ... Detective?"

He noticed a chair behind him. He took it and drug it toward her; the steel-legs screeching in a painful harmony. She drew back as he brought it around her, positioning it so that it faced where he'd been looming. "Sit down."

"What?" she muttered nonplussed.

"*I said, SIT DOWN!*"

She couldn't have obeyed any faster. For a moment, there was only his silent glare aimed down at her. He was eyeing her the way a wolf might eye a smaller, more fragile creature; maybe one already injured, without any hope of escape. Cold and calculating.

Then he went back to the phone. He took hold and ripped it from its base in the wall, letting it drop to the floor with a resounding crash. Joan jumped in the chair and gave a silent scream; suddenly her throat was tight and dry and she came to the dreadful realization that she *couldn't* scream.

He was moving towards her. Shuffling slowly, thoughtfully, as though each sway of his body were deliberate. Suddenly he paused. Noticing something by the stove. He chuckled and cocked his thumb to the wall, where a dartboard hung. "Doubt the health inspector would approve of this." He stepped aside and took something from his side pocket.

Joan could see it was a knife. A switchblade.

He pressed a button and six-inches of brilliant, menacing steel shot from the contraption. Joan was sure she'd caught a glimpse of her own terrified, black-eyed reflection.

He drew his arm back and flung the knife as casually as a pitcher might a fastball; it spun once in the air and stabbed into the board, rocking it. He'd missed the bullseye by maybe an inch.

A sob escaped Joan before she could stop it. Silent and painful.

He sneered at her. She couldn't believe she'd thought him a handsome man, before. It was so clear now ... what was behind that face. The face of a killer.

From his other side pocket, came another knife, identical to the other except for its bone-hued handle. He ejected the blade and almost immediately hurled it at the board. The same skilled, laxed, launch with the same precise graceful spin – this time it jabbed dead-center, right above the last, at a downward angle. Almost as though he'd been several feet taller when he'd thrown it.

Joan's tears began to burn and her throat began to ache. He was laughing at her. Cruel, maniacal laughter filled with stark, sadistic pleasure deriving from the palpable terror emitting from the waitress.

He tugged his knives from the wall, the punctured cork giving no resistance. He took the black one, folded it shut, and dropped it back into his coat pocket.

The other knife he kept open. Its blade gleaming as he moved toward her. Coming closer. That horrible smile. That eerie flicker of exhilaration in his eyes. He wanted to hurt her. No. He wanted to kill her.

Though she knew this, she found herself unable to move. Unable to force the numbness of her legs to lessen and unable to smother the paralyzing trepidation that came at the idea of making a run for it. The world was a hazy dreamland. A nightmare gliding closer.

Just feet away, the madman raised his blade so that it was in between them. So that they could both admire its shiny, murderous potential. When he spoke, his words cut into her, much the way that knife soon would: "The hours have felt like days ... the weeks, eternities ... you don't know the hunger that's festered inside of me waiting for our moment together ... but the moments finally come, Joan ... I've waited for this..."

"I know you have, Rowker," a voice came from the shadows.

The killer froze. Now he was the one who looked unsure. Afraid. "WHO'S THERE? WHO SAID THAT? COME OUT! COME OUT OR *I'LL KILL YOU!*"

Joan jumped in her seat, but not because of the psychotic screaming, but because when the voice spoke again it came from behind her. "You won't be doing anymore killing, Rowker. It's over."

The killer stepped back as the shadow-figure turned to man. Joan's frightened, unbelieving eyes widened. "John?" He put a hand on her shoulder, but never took his eyes from the knife-wielding maniac he was calling, Rowker. "I've brought someone with me, Rowker. You've read about him. You might've noticed him at some point tonight, too. Lieutenant."

From the darkness, another shadow came into light. This one larger but equally familiar. It was the drunk who'd spent the evening putting away shots of coffee and nodding in and out of consciousness at the counter. The same drunk who'd gone stumbling out after someone she'd thought was a detective. Only now he wasn't drunk. Now his expression was hard, and painfully sober. Without slurring, he said, "He's right, Rowker. It's all over. You're coming with us." Three shadows soon followed from behind him. Glinting badges pinned to uniforms made each of the officers stand out.

"This is Lieutenant Brody. We've been looking for you. You're terribly sick, Rowker. You need to let us take you somewhere where they can help you. You can't go on like this."

The killer wasn't listening. He was shaking his head, his face entangled with a wild mix of hostile panic and incredulity. "...how ... how ... you were *waiting!*"

"When I lost her, I had plenty of time to worry about what might happen. Especially when Brody told me how you slipped away from him in a car. I knew then, with her missing and you roaming around playing detective, there was the real possibility that everything had fouled-up, and that you could've gotten to her. There's a dragnet going on out there for you, Rowker. But knowing how familiar you'd made yourself with this place, I had a hunch you'd take her here for some privacy. I knew she'd left her key behind, and that led to plenty of second guessing ... time felt eternal for me too. But when I heard the lock on the door shimmying, I knew you were here–"

The killer brought his arm back, and now Joan found she could scream. She screamed because she knew he was throwing the knife. And where.

John cut the monologue short, cut-off by Joan's' shrieking and the quick understanding that he was about to hurl his knife; but the killer wasn't focused on him – he was focused on Joan.

The knife came spinning from across the room. Joan unconsciously stood, but it was too late. The blade stuck into Johns gut as he rushed to shield Joan.

He grunted out in pain and crumpled to the floor, in Joan's arms. From behind, all the policemen had drawn their revolvers, and one of the uniforms let off a shot. The bullet strafed off a piece of the wall as Rowker ducked back into the dining room just in time.

"*Get him!*" Brody commanded, stopping to see if John was still alive.

He ordered one of the uniforms to stay behind and he rushed after the others. The room was empty, the front door easing shut; a uniform appeared suddenly, he shook his head. Brody growled and looked right as another door opened. The other officer appeared. "He went out the bathroom window! He's bookin' it across the street!"

They followed him out and to the other side of the street, lined with apartment buildings. Dozens of uniforms and plainclothesmen were emerging from alleys, building entrances, and cars from all over the street. "He's goin' up the fire escape!" Brody exclaimed, using his revolver to point out the building the shadow was climbing. The hasty figure was already halfway up.

Brody, as an older, heavier man fell behind the younger, more fit patrolmen who were rushing the stairs two at a time.

The first two to make it to the roof: a young detective who'd been closest to the building, and a blonde uniform who'd actually lost his cap while darting up the stairs. There was no one in sight. "You take in between the coops, I'll go around the left," said the detective. The blonde-cop nodded and started into the alley of pigeon coops; his .38 special aimed ahead.

His palms were clammy, and he began to worry that his gun would slip from his grasp if he had to use it.

There was a springing sound, and he knew that he was in trouble. He stepped aside, but the knife had already plunged into his back as the killer leaped from atop a pen, striking from behind; the officer fired a blind round as the painful weight and pressure of the attack brought him down. The madman didn't let-up right away. The cop could feel him making sure the blade was as far into his back as it could be.

And then there were voices and the killer ran. Leaving a polished black-handle protruding from the prostrate policeman. The detective was back around the crates and rushing to the wounded officer; Brody and three others made it to the roof.

They knelt beside him, not daring to touch the weapon. "Get an ambulance up here, right now," Brody dictated to no-one in particular. "Which way, son?"

The blonde officer pointed his revolver down the alley. Managing to grunt out, "Straight ahead."

"Stay with him." Another aimless demand before continuing forward.

At the end of the roof there was nothing. No killer, and no second fire escape. No more pigeon coops to hide behind.

The Slayer had vanished.

And then Brody saw it. "Jesus." A white blanket. Billowing gracefully as it fluttered to the courtyard six-stories below. A man's hat twirled along with it. "That crazy bastard." Another piece of linen went soaring as the figure struggled across the highest clothesline. "Jesus, come on." The young detective and the lone uniform followed the lieutenant as he worked himself onto the nearest balcony. A good four-foot drop from the roof.

The line shook as Rowker inched his way carefully to the other building. Swatting away any laundry in his way.

"How the hell is it holding him?" the uniform spoke incredulously.

"It isn't," said Brody.

Almost at once they all saw what he meant. The wheel operating the clothesline, drilled into the bricks just outside the railing, had begun to bend outward. Every few seconds the screws would screech a little farther out. The bottom two slower than the top. "Jesus. Hold it!"

All three held the straining device; knowing it wouldn't do any good.

About seventeen-feet above the sidewalk in between the buildings, Rowker began to tire. He was losing the hold he had with his feet. Trying to wrap them back around the wire, he noticed the police had followed to the balcony. But they weren't looking at him. They were busy messing with something. Something where the clothesline he'd wormed across, began.

Suddenly the line dropped a few inches. He hugged onto the thin rope tighter. Another few inches went. Desperation and desolation washed over him in nauseous waves.

He knew what they were doing now.

He looked ahead to the other building. No-one was there to hold that wheel.

"It isn't fai – "The wheel ripped from the far-building and the Slayer fell from the sky. Screaming. His arms moving wildly, reaching for something to catch that wasn't there. His legs hit another one of the lines on his way down, and he went spinning. Hitting head-first just over the border of grass into concrete.

The death of his screams and the reverberations of his body cracking against the earth filled the night. Shadows of police officers surrounded the still-figure sprawled out down below. Brody could see most had their guns drawn, covering the figure laying in a growing pool of what was black this high in the night, while a few kept their weapons lowered.

They knew Rowker wasn't going anywhere.

Seven

They were sitting in the back of an ambulance. She was wrapped in a blanket, while he was having his stomach patched up. At one point, two men-in-white sauntered by carrying a stretcher. The white-blanket draped over its cargo already splotched in red.

Joan held her breath as they passed.

"Well he stuck you pretty good, but he didn't hit anything too important. Just the fleshy-part here."

"Good thing he was in a hurry, huh, Doc?"

"I'll say. It's alright, for now. But you need to come with me to the hospital."

Brody approached then, hands buried in his pockets; his expression softened to a man whose job was done. "How you doin', Conte?"

"I guess I'll live. How about your boy on the roof?"

"Well he'll be off the beat for'a while, but I think he'll pull through." The lieutenant went on. "Don't tell anyone I said this ... but you ain't so bad, Conte. You and your nutty ideas. Take care of him, miss." Then he turned and ambled away before anyone could say something back.

"Conte, huh?" said Joan. "Where have I heard that name before?"

He only grinned at her, amused.

And then it came to her. "You ... you're the paperman ... you're the one who wrote that article ... the *same one* we were talking about!"

His grin widened. "Fred Conte. But my good friends call me, Freddy."

"Well listen here, Mr. Conte—"

"Didn't you hear me? I said my good friends call me—"

"I heard you," she snapped.

He frowned at her.

"I don't understand anything that's happened tonight. What're you doing here? What was with the slip of paper that fell from your jacket?"

He smiled again. "Yea, I knew that was what chased you off. Bet you thought that was a record of your schedule, didn't you?"

She nodded.

"You should have used those beautiful brown-eyes to look harder at those notes. If you had, you would've noticed the arrival and departure times wouldn't add up to you.

"Want to guess who might've stopped by most days, about twenty-minutes at a time?"

She suddenly knew. "Him."

"He's name was Kyle Rowker. Just one of four suspects Brody and his boys were considering. All of them live right here, in Dunbar. Rowker knew they were onto him. He also knew they weren't sure. I'd been following the case, and when the attacks suddenly stopped after Rowker got wise – I started following him. When he started spending his days frequenting the diner, I had a feeling he was getting antsy. That was the only place he'd ever show his face more than once. I knew if he felt like he had any kind of a break ... he'd slip up.

"That's why I planted that article."

"You *planted* it?"

"The whole piece was bogus. I told Brody about my idea for that bit of fiction. Something to make him think we had nothing but bad info. Brody had his eyes set on Rowker, too, and he thought he'd make a move, just like I did."

"So, you knew he was going to try... try and kill me?"

His eyes narrowed and he spoke carefully. "I knew it was someone at Fritz' diner being watched. Someone who spent their days there. But not who. Then tonight, when I finally went inside ... and saw you ... I knew who was in trouble."

Joan tried not to smile, but couldn't help herself. "What ... what about the song?"

"You mean, our song?"

"I..."

"I heard him listening to it a few times. It was too sweet a song for someone like him to know. I figured he got it from ... well, now I know it was from you."

"Well ... thank you, Mr. Conte. For saving my life. Even if you did have a hand in endangering it."

"You mean, Thank you Freddy."

"You know, I think this has finally given me the best reason I need to leave the city."

"Leave the city?" he repeated grimly.

"I've been thinking of leaving for a while. Now, I'm sure it's right."

"Can't anything be done to change you mind?"

"I don't think—"

But he was already kissing her. And she found herself letting him.

"...well ... maybe..."

IV

Devil's Gypsy

Well, goin' pretty fast, looked behind
A-Hear come the Devil doin' ninty-nine
I said,
Move, hot-rod, move man
Move, hot-rod, move man
Move hot-rod, move me on down the line!

    -   Gene Vincent's "Race with the Devil"

It was a dreary night; foggy. The moon just visible through a vast, sailing cloud, acting as a sort of transparent-veil with an everlasting rip in its' seam, spilling what little light it would. But even the dull night couldn't hide them. Not when they moved through the street like that; like a pack of wolves in leather jackets. What the cold light of the moon couldn't illuminate, the streetlights did.

From down the sidewalk, a silver-haired woman who'd been escorting two small children in the opposite direction, suddenly took a firm hold to each, dragging them into the closest business with an open door. From the adjacent curb, a young couple decided to take the long way through a dark alley, they moved hastily. In a passing window, a barber was sweeping away the evenings' trimmings when he noticed them; but suddenly the floor was clean enough and he hurried to the back of the store. Not that any of them knew – or cared to – but from behind, the driver of an approaching Buick had just begun to place his hand against the cars horn, only to have his worried-face female-companion quickly jerk it away. He did not try again. Only pulled to the curb and waited.

They moved through the street with a sort of imperial stride; there was no urgency in their movement. Formidably identical in most ways, they were all young, healthy looking men with greasy, styled-hair. Most had their collars turned up. They were all sporting pegged jeans or chinos, and aside from the few in Converses, they were all in motorcycle boots.

Another thing. Leather or not, each one of their jackets were black, and each had the same, sizable-patch proudly displayed on their backs. A red, sneering Devil face was the only color to the jacket; the face had a sharp, sinister goatee with a waxed-looking mustache. A cigarette hung loosely from its fangs, a thin trail of smoke lead-up between two curved-horns.

Above the face, in white, easily-legible cursive font, read, *"The Devil's Gypsies."*

Voodoo Vic was up front, ahead of the others, but not in the lead. No, that spot was reserved for Steady Jack, just as it always was; the leader of the Gypsies, with the icy nerve of a ghost. Steady as a rock. Unwavering. That was what everyone said. Vic always wondered. He finished flattening the back-half of his pompadour and slipped the comb into his pants, careful not to drop it in the right pocket; that pocket was for his blade. He could still feel the lead-pipe, secure in his waistband, concealed by the flap of his jacket.

Steady Jack had made it clear at the meeting that it was to be a No-Weapon Rumble; agreed to by The Fourth Avenuers. Vic had protested; said that it was stupid to take their word for anything. Hop-Along had been first to jump on board – just like he always was when Vic suggested something – but some of the others had begun to agree before being overruled on the matter. So that was to be *that*, but *that* didn't stop Vic from sticking the pipe down his pants on the way out of the club. No one had seen him but Hop-Along, and of

course he'd wanted to pack one, too, but Vic told him
no.

Now, Hop-Along Garzara was marching along to
his right – like he always was – his short legs doing
their best to keep up with the older boys. To his right,
and well into the next lane, was the rest of the gang:
Puffing away at an L&M was Chaz Chains, looking
lonely and uncertain without his motorcycle chain to
spin in the air. Next to him was Right Hook Rocco, a
former youth boxer who'd earned his name by
demonstrating his gym training more than once in a
brawl. Then there was Marco The Martian, passing his
flask back and forth; his corn-colored hair cut strangely
close at the top for how long and greased back the sides
were; by far, he had the longest and pointiest sideburns
of the bunch, he was also the only one sporting a denim
jacket. Next to him was Sick 'Em Sully, looking hard-
eyed and limber, with both thumbs hooked in the loops
of his jeans. After Chubs McNeil (the biggest and
slowest gang member in the street) there was Bolo
Billy; fastened around his sports shirt was a string-tie
with the silver-scorpion piece he always wore.

The Devil's Gypsies rounded a street corner and
started across Fourth Avenue. They were close. Vic was
ready. He was always ready, he hated Avenuers; they
were weak-jives who never left their turf. Vic could
never understand why they didn't just smash them all
and take the Avenue for themselves. The mouth of the
alley they were heading for came into view, deliberately
chosen for the extra space it provided.

No weapons, he scoffed again silently. Next, we'll
be bringing in a referee.

Vic remembered when things used to be different;
at least that's what his brother had always told him. In
the Good Ol' Days, street beefs – as long as they had
not become so personal that one wanted the other dead

– were settled on the road. Each gang would pick their best driver, set them up in their sweetest ride, and drag it out. Shame had been the ultimate cost then; at least until the roads were torn apart, redone, and rerouted.

Until, Dead Man's Curve.

Near the top of Smokey Joe Mountain, not so far down the line of the winding-road, there was now a rounding so sudden, so sharp, and so high in the sky it affectively put an end to all local hot-rodding. The neighboring county of Barnett now had the only roads worth racing that you didn't have to worry about plummeting off.

A young Gyp named Razor Ritchie had been The Curve's final casualty, and had since become a part of gang folklore. Ritchie had been racing against an infamous dragster named Doogan; he and his three, two-barrel carburetors were known throughout the state, drifting from town to town, cleaning guys out. Ritchie had been waiting for him, he'd even gone out of state to swipe a 550 Spyder for the race; ominously enough the same car James Dean would later bite it in. During, Ritchie had apparently taken advantage of Doogan slowing down at The Curve, and, fearing shame more than death, gunned it, overestimating the drift and crashing through the guard rail. The car went thrashing down the hill, shredding into a thousand different pieces before finally exploding.

Ironically, a shameful stigma had surrounded The Gypsies since then; the gang who started and reigned over the races before losing everything in its' finale. His brother had often told him – long before any man in a suit had rallied for more war in Asia – that that meant *they all* had something to prove. Vic had always taken that to heart. Especially after his brother was gone.

The shadows of the wide alley swallowed them as they moved in, the only light provided by the moon that seemed to have come out of hiding to give them light to fight by. It seemed for a moment they were alone. And then several silhouettes took shape down the alley, growing taller as they moved toward them. Vic cracked his knuckles and imagined the slick-licks of a guitar strumming; he couldn't help himself, he heard Link Wray in his head every time there was a rumble coming.

The figures stepped into the light in the center of the alley; one gang in black, the other in yellow windbreakers with a single white stripe on each left sleeve. As with The Gypsies, there was a lead man of The Avenuers; he took a step closer, smirking, a single, greasy lock hung between his eyes. "Jackie Boy! What took you so long? We was startin' to wonder."

Steady Jack cocked his head back, looking first to Sick 'Em Sully, then at the others; The Gypsies broke into a resounding roar of laughter. Jack dug into his pocket and came back out with a five-spot he passed directly to Sully. "Hell Chip, I didn't think you'd show. Even lost a bet over it."

"We wouldn't miss this for—"

"No," Jack interrupted, "I mean you personally, Chip. I didn't think *you'd* show. Sully thought you'd stick your head out, say somethin' dumb, then peel out before you broke a nail."

"You ain't so lucky, Jackie," Chip said, the amused look in his eyes gone, replaced with something else. "Now are we gonna dance or sweet-talk all night?"

"Thought you'd never ask."

Steady Jack and Avenue Chip started to slowly circle each other, knees bent, fists tightening. The rest of the gang members spread out, each approaching a rival as though it had been organized that way. Voodoo Vic went with one of the Aves he recognized; he was one of the stockier of the gang, but Vic remembered seeing him in a foot-cast the previous year. He thought he could stomp his ankle, crack him one, then move on to another. He wouldn't even need the piece to start with. The glow from the sky began to weaken, and down the way an alley-cat toppled over a trash-ben, scurrying away.

It started as though there'd been a que. Chip swung first, but Jack caught the blow under his arm and jabbed his elbow into Chip's ear; he went stumbling back in pain, but took advantage of the closeness and dragged Jack with him. They took their fight against a dumpster while the rest of them sprung; snarling, kicking, clawing, biting, and wrestling like wild animals. Right Hook used his name-sake to clock his rival right in the jaw; he flopped to the ground, instantly defeated. Rocco moved on to help Marco, who'd tripped and was being kicked down the alley by his opponent. Bolo Billy seemed to be playing with his rival, ducking and shifting his jabs and laughing and taunting him about not being able to hit the side of a barn, before socking him just enough to draw blood and antagonize him some more. Chubs and Sick 'Em had switched; after Chubs tossed the Avenuer against the alley wall, Sully ran over and started kicking him before he could stand. Before he could stop this, the other Ave was into it with Chubs, who was absorbing every blow, only to lift the slimmer-boy up and toss him against the wall as well. This happened a few times, and each time the Yellow Jacket would get back up, shake his head in a daze, and head back to start the process all over again. Hop-Along had tried to stay close to Vic, but the Avenuer he was tangling with was getting the better of him, easily defecting his punches and landing his own torso shots, sending a sick regurgitation up Garzara's throat. But he couldn't stop. Couldn't let them see him fall.

Vic found he didn't even need to re-break the guy's ankle. He caught the Ave with a solid, deep jab-hook combo; first the gut, then the chin. The Avenuer recoiled, but in the wrong direction and was quickly snatched up by Chubs.

Vic could see Hop-Along wasn't doing so well, despite doing his best to hold his own. But before he could move that way, a whistle escaped between the Avenues leader's split lips. Suddenly there were more shadows coming from down the alley, and when they came into the light, each yellow stripe on the sleeves of the white windbreakers stood out. Recruits. Five of them.

"*You cheap weasel!*" Jack growled before starting in on Chip again.

Most of The Gypsies looked alarmed and gathered closer. But Vic moved toward them, a lead-pipe seemed to have appeared in his hand. He was shouting, "*Come on! Yea, yea, come on!* You're nothin' I wasn't ready for!" The sound of the pipe banging against the stone of the alley floor went cracking into the night like a gunshot. "*Come on then!*"

The young, Aspiring-Avenuers glanced uncertainly from one another, spreading out, creeping in. When the first one struck, Vic brought the pipe down on his knee. He cried out and collapsed as the others jumped. Three of them moved as if they were going to rush him, coming closer despite each wild swing of the instrument. That was when the fourth leaped onto Vic's back. They rushed him then, but Vic had already gone stumbling blindly backwards, colliding with the wall. The boy crumpled from his back to the ground. He saw that two of the recruits had been pulled into a separate fight with Sully and Rocco, but one was still coming at him; an open blade in his hand. "You *bashed* my knee!" he cried out.

"Your face is next."

The Avenuer took a stab at him so suddenly he nearly stuck Vic's ribs. Just barley managing to dodge the stabbing, Vic took hold of the boy's sleeve and brought the pipe down on his knife-wielding hand. He let him drop to his knees, screaming. Holding his twisted, mangled fingers out in front of him. Around them, the fighting had stopped.

Above, the moon played its' shadow games once more and the frightened, tortured face of the Avenuer was blacked out as Vic brought the pipe back down. The vibrations of the pipes' impact sent a tremor up his arms. He heard metal scraping and he thought the Ave was going for his blade again. Another swing. Another judder.

He swung again but suddenly there was nothing to hit. He took a few more swings in the dark before the moonlight peeked back out, and exposed the sprawling, bloody mess.

"...Holy shit..." a voice said.

Vic looked to the pipe still in his hand; drops of blood were dribbling off it like a leaky faucet, specking the white windbreaker below with tiny, red dots. How many times had he hit him? He couldn't remember.

"Let's get the hell out of here," Chip shouted, limping away with the rest of his gang back down the alley.

The Devil's Gypsies gathered around the body. Hop-Along shuffled over, rubbing his jaw. "You alright?" he asked Vic; he didn't answer. His attention hadn't left the dripping pipe.

"You stupid asshole," said Jack. "You stupid ... *stupid...*"

Bolo: "Think they'll rat?"

"Hell yes, they'll rat," said Rocco.

Sick 'Em: "Cops'll round up everyone they can after they find him. Avenuers too. Yea, they'll spill."

Chubs: "All of us?"

Martian: "Hell yes, all of us!"

"...stupid..." Jack continued.

The clouds had moved on. It was as though the body were *supposed* to be seen.

Chaz: "Is he? Is he de–"

Bolo: "Shit yea, look at his face! What's left of it."

"We've gotta go," said Jack.

They all seemed to be waiting for Vic. He had a strange, enigmatic blankness about him. They couldn't tell if he was catatonically disturbed or exhilaratingly fascinated. Finally Hop-Along got his attention and they skulked out of the alley. "I think we won," Vic muttered, breaking into a lope with the rest of them.

~ ~ ~

Steady Jack was the proud owner of a jet black '57 Ford Fairlaner. And even though the races were gone, it was a ride envied by all. But none coveted that car quite the way Voodoo Vic did, and now, sitting in the passenger's seat styling the greasy ducktail of his hair, discreetly parked behind the diner, he found it provided a sort of comfort; fueling the apathy he was beginning to feel regarding his imminent outlaw status. Hop-Along sat in the back while Jack leaned against the car outside, standing guard. It was nearly midnight.

From around the diner, Marco Martian and Chubs came ambling toward them carefully. "Words out, alright," said Martian. "They ain't sayin' how, but it must have been The Avenuers who sang, because they're lookin' for Voodoo."

Vic stopped combing his hair and raised his lip in a snarl. "Those squealin' crumbs. I'll–"

"We'll take care of them," Jack cut in. "You just gotta stay out of sight 'till we can get you a carpet-ride out of town." He looked back to Marco. "Did the Ave croak?"

"I don't think so. But it's bad. They ain't givin' too many details. Just that he was still in surgery."

"Guess he won't be getting his yellow windbreaker," Vic said from the car, while Hop-Along snickered in the backseat.

"Jesus. What a damn mess." Jack went on. "Alright, you two get back to The Spot and shut the clubhouse down. Get the rest of the boys and beat it over to Milton Hills Inn. Tell Gunther I need a favor in the form of a room. Kick back there and wait for me."

"And what do you want me to do, hide in the sewers?" said Vic.

"I want you to keep your head in a hole 'till the heat looks the other way long enough for you to boogie out of here."

"Where do I start diggin'?"

"I got a place. You just sit there and try not to fuck anything else up." Jack sauntered to the phone booth, jingling the change in his Levi's.

Vic lit a cigarette and felt the smooth touch of the steering wheel. Damn, he loved this car.

~ ~ ~

Percy Watkin, the thirty-one-year-old mechanic and part garage owner – and most importantly, Devil's Gypsy associate – answered his door at nearly one in the morning to three toughs in leather jackets. After he let them in, he had his girlfriend take two of them into the kitchen for coffee; the taller one said he'd take a soda pop and followed her, while Percy took Jack aside. "You know I wanna help you out anyway I can, Jack. But this won't be for long, will it? They say that kid in the hospital is in pretty-bad shape. If he dies, there'll be three times as many cops out, kicking in doors, pulling raids. If I got pinched with *him* here I could lose my business."

"Stay cool, Percy. I just need time to find him a way to burrow out of town before *that* comes. Tomorrow night, at the latest." Jack took some bills from his pocket and handed a few over to Percy.

Percy stuffed them in his robe and said, "What about the little one?"

"Who? Hop-Along?" Jack smiled. "Don't worry. He's like a dog that can talk. He goes where Vic goes. He won't give you trouble. Just keep them inside and don't let anyone in."

"Anything else?"

"Yea." Jack pointed to the kitchen door. "Don't give him too much sugar; you don't want to see him when he gets excited."

Early the next morning Percy called the garage and told them he was sick and wouldn't be in that day. After that he decided to sleep in. A few hours later, he lumbered out of his bedroom to find his guests where he'd left them; at the kitchen table. The ashtray from the den had been moved there and already had a mountain of smashed butts going, and the portable radio from his roll-top desk was beside it, half-blaring rock 'n roll. Aside from his girlfriend, Jessica, Percy also lived with his two younger cousins; one of them was leaning against the counter, while the other sat opposite the others at the table, listening intently to whatever he was being told. Some sort of paper was spread out on the table.

Promptly, Jessica marched over to Percy; he always noticed how her lips looked thinner when she was angry or nervous. "About time," she snapped quietly.

"What's going on?"

"Go see for yourself what your friends are talking about doing." She strutted out of the kitchen then. Past the door, Percy heard her mutter, "I didn't know it was the James Gang we were entertaining."

Tightening his robe, Percy loomed over the table. He could see now that the paper on the table was actually the cleaned-off inside of a burger wrapper. Some sort of one-dimensionally crude design had been scribbled onto it. Various, tiny squares made up the inside of this design; the first box he saw was labeled *ENTRANCE*, the next *SIDE ENTRANCE*. Finally, at the back, in the biggest squares, *CAGES*, and behind that, *VAULT*.

"What the hell is this?"

"Got a caper in the works." His cousin smiled up to him. Percy noticed his hair was combed straight back in a way it had never been before, and his tee-shirt sleeves were rolled up; in one, there was even the bulge of a cigarette pack.

"*What?*" Percy spit out, his voice became shrill and his eyes widened the way they often did when confronted with incredulity.

"Don't worry," Vic finally spoke. "You're in for a cut. We'll all be fixed after this."

Percy rubbed the crust out of his eyes and looked to the clock on the counter. "It's only eleven-thirty in the morning, and you're telling me that you've already got some kind of ... *robbery* planned out? Aren't you supposed to be playing dead?" He was talking to Vic; who did not look amused.

"He got the idea last night, after you crashed," his new greaser cousin informed him with the same stroke of enthusiasm. "Figured he'd need dough no matter where he went on the lam. Makes sense to me. Hop-Along already went out to stake the place. Had to leave the Jacket here of course, but he got the whole layout of the bank–"

"...I ... I..." Percy stuttered. "When are you planning on doing this?"

"We're goin' later today," said Vic.

"...I ... I still can't believe it! What're you going to knock them over with, the pipe you used to beat that kid?"

Vic looked to him for the first time that morning and shot to his feet, his chair went screeching out, balancing on its' back legs. Percy took a full step back. "I take care of my friends, Perc. And I stomp everyone else. Just keep being my friend." He sat back down, and when he spoke, it was directed to the others. "As far as artillery goes, forget it. Bolo's old mans' got that gun cage at his place; couple of shotguns, .351 rifles..."

Hop-Along spoke up, "How can we be sure Billy will let us have them?"

"He's a Gyp, ain't he? Why wouldn't he? Besides, Perc's got that .45 from the Army. Ain't that right, Perc?" now Vic was smiling at him.

Percy glared down at his cousin, but he wouldn't look at him. He knew he likely hadn't meant any harm in bragging about the gun. Just that. Bragging. But he still wanted to smack him.

"How many cashiers were working the place?" Vic asked Hop-Along.

Percy left his kitchen and went to hide in his bedroom. His head was swimming, and all he could think about was that he shouldn't have slept in. He'd have plenty of time to sleep in lockup.

~ ~ ~

It was nearly sundown. Percy had broken his promise to Jack by letting Vic and Hop-Along out of the house (he wasn't counting when the little one went out while he slept) to go see about the guns for the bank heist. He needed the privacy. He gathered his housemates into the kitchen. "Now look. I hate to have Jack mad at us, but he'll just have to understand. This fellow is crossing a line. And don't think for a second you're going on that caper!" he spoke to the eldest cousin. "Now I'm going to ask him to leave, immediately."

"What if he won't go?" said Jessica.

"Why wouldn't he?" Percy felt dumb immediately after asking this.

"Because he's insane, obviously."

"I think she's right," the younger cousin weighed in. "You should at least keep the automatic on you in case he gets fresh when you break it to him."

They all agreed, even after some reluctance from the elder cousin. They filed into the den and Percy went to open the desk drawer he kept the gun in. Only when he looked inside it was gone.

He heard a pistol cocking, and turned around to see Vic in the doorway.

"Told you, Hop," Vic growled, raising the .45 higher above his waist. "House full'a squares. Guess it's good for me we stuck around, huh?"

"Now look," Percy started, certain he was about to be shot with his own gun. "This is too much. Even for Jack–"

"Forget Jack, you were trying to screw me. And after I was gonna cut you in for full-shares of the bank-take." He shook his head wistfully.

"You're going overboard, Vic," Percy persisted carefully. "You've already got a murder-cloud hanging over your head, and now you're talking about pushing in a bank. What happens if you do go in there, Vic? You'll just end-up knocking off some other poor bastard and they'll have enough to fry you and everyone around."

"I can stick up that bank without killing anyone."

"I'm not so sure." The others moved behind Percy. Something was going on in Vic's eyes. He looked ... almost pleased. Percy kept on. "You're out of control. That's why you're in this jam. You can't sto—"

He was cut off when Vic strode across the room and rapped the butt of the gun against Percy's head. A thin stream of blood came from his temple, his eyes rolling in his head. He collapsed at the feet of the others. Jessica was screaming when Vic's cold-glare trailed up to them. In one swift, deliberate motion, he aimed the gun at their feet and jerked its' slid back; spitting out a loose bullet that hit Jessica right between the eyes. The pitch of her scream went higher, and she grasped onto the shirts of each of the cousins. Vic was laughing.

When he was done amusing himself he ordered them to drag Percy along and to get into the closet, locking them in with a key he'd swiped from the desk along with the gun. While he had Hop-Along rummaged the place for cash and jewelry, he knocked on the closet door with the gun. He could hear muffled sobs. "Can ya hear me? I know Perc is probably still sleeping, but when he wakes up tell him I was perfectly able to heist *this* place without killing anybody. At least so far. Keep still in there."

After that they swiped the keys to Percy's truck and left for the Garzara home. It seemed Vic couldn't help but burn-out as they pulled away. Tires screamed and rubber burned, and then the Gypsies went speeding off down the road.

~ ~ ~

Hop-Along had not seen either of his parents since he was seven. He lived in a studio apartment with his older sister, Lily Garzara. Vic had never met Lily before. Vic had never even heard of Lily before; he wasn't sure if anyone had.

She was immensely pretty. Young, in her twenties maybe, but no older than twenty-one. She had the bluest eyes, and strawberry blonde hair that was pulled up, emphasizing her sharp cheekbones. Vic could tell that she wasn't happy with her brother for bringing him there, though it didn't seem that she knew *who* he was or *what* he'd done. She was hospitable enough, offering him coffee or milk. "Soda pop," he said.

They sat on the divan – the only piece of furniture in the room, and she brought them both cokes. She asked Hop-Along a few questions about his day; he answered vaguely before getting up and leaving, saying he had to make a phone call. There was brief silence Lily tried to fill by asking Vic if he was from the neighborhood. He said yes and smiled at her. He kept smiling at her. And there was something in his eyes that made her decide she was finished with the small talk. "Well, I've got any early morning. Think I'll get ready for bed. Goodnight."

He didn't answer her. But he was still smiling. She went down the hall, stopping just before going into her bedroom to see him still watching her. She shut the door.

Hop-Along came out of the kitchen then, not saying anything, just sticking out his thumb and pinky finger by his head in the "telephone" gesture. Vic got up to answer. "Yea?"

"You *stupid...*"

"Hi Jack."

"I really thought there wasn't any way you could've made things worse. Percy was a Friend of Ours. Christ sake, where the hell do you think we fence all those boosted car parts?"

"Forget them *and* that. I got a sweet score set-up and–"

"Score?" Jack repeated. "What fucking score? You know something, Voodoo? I think you've flipped your lid. Seems like you forgot who the Head Devil is."

"Now listen, Jack, I'm tellin' you–"

"No, I'm telling *you*: if you have any brains left you'll kick-back 'til I get there. Later, after dark. Stay *right there*." He spoke these last two words in slow emphasis. And then he was gone. Vic wanted to smash the phone down in its cradle; wanted to rip its' cord from the wall and chuck it through the window. Who did Jack think he was? Taking sides with outsiders over a Devil. Unheard of, and *he* was the one supposed to be in trouble? He found his composure when he remembered the bank. He didn't need any one's help. Hop-Along could wait in the car while he knocked the place over all on his own. Why not? If anyone gave him static he'd drop them and move on. Sack up and get out. Simple.

"Hell yes I'm still in," was Hop-Along's reply when Vic asked about the bank job.

"Good. We've got about an hour before the bank closes; that mean's as few faces as possible. I need you to go boost a car. A fast one. Perc's truck just won't cut-it."

"What about you?"

"I'm gonna try and get in touch with Bolo about the guns."

Hop-Along did something he'd never done before. He didn't say okay. He didn't say anything. His eyes were full of questions, full of uncertainty.

"Go on, before the bank closes."

In a slow stride he put his Club Jacket back on, and moved to the door, looking to Vic one more time with that air of confoundment. And then he left.

Vic took a long, final drag of his cigarette before dropping it down the neck of the soda bottle. There was an unframed mirror hanging from the wall; Vic stopped and carefully combed his hair. And then he went down the hallway.

The light on the other side of the room framed the door against the darkness. Outside the sun was departing. The night came early with the season.

When he got to the door he saw that it was slightly ajar; when his fingers touched it, it crept a bit further open. The blackness covered his peeking-eye as he watched Lily at her mirror, brushing her mass of hair that had been let down past her shoulders. She'd changed clothes. Now she was in a silk negligee, almost see-through; like the ones the Paris girls wore in those magazines his brother used to give him, long before going overseas to have his head blown-off by some stranger in a foreign uniform.

When this thought came to him, he found he'd already started into her room. She rose, startled, pulling her robe tighter. "What're you doing in here?"

Vic didn't answer her. "I wonder why Hop-Along never told us about you."

"If you mean Arthur, then I don't know, you'd have to ask him." She crossed her arms as he came closer.

"You know, I'm not going to be in town much longer."

"Oh?"

"I'll have plenty of dough, too."

"I'm glad for you. Why are you telling me?"

"I want you to come with me."

Her face went tight. She was still very attractive to him. Even when she was scared.

"What about it?"

"I don't even know you."

"So? I like what I see. Don't you?"

"You think you're really something, don't you?"

"Don't you?"

"I think you're a criminal."

"So? What's wrong with that?"

"Nothing. But it's not for me."

"I think it could be." He was so close the scent of pomade was abundant, she could even smell a hint of after-shave; but it was faint, he mostly smelled like someone who smoked like a chimney.

"I don't think so.

"Try again." He drew her to him, roughly, and forced her lips to his. After a second she pushed him away.

"I said no thank you."

"I said try again."

Before he could pull her back she slapped him. He turned back to her and something happened. His eyes became darker; brooding and lazy. She was certain he'd grab her and kiss her rougher then, but what he did was belt her.

She dropped to the floor, holding her mouth. When she looked into her palm there was blood. He towered over her. Her robe had come undone in the fall, and she could see his eyes rising about her legs in lecherous inches. She was crawling backwards as he stepped to her.

"What the fuck are you doing?"

Vic's glare shot to the doorway; Hop-Along was standing there. Vic ran his hands over his hair once and said, "What're you doing here? I told you – "

"What am *I* doing here?" Hop-Along repeated incredulously. "What the fuck are *you* doing here?" He ambled across the room. His destination obvious.

"Look, Hop, it ain't–" But Hop lunged at him. Vic flipped his jacket, going for the gun, but before Hop-Along could reach him, Lily had jumped on Vic's back; beating and scratching wildly at his head and face. The gun slipped from his hand to the floor. Hop-Along had reached him and the three were now wrestling and tumbling and spinning around the room, crashing into the bed and spilling over on the floor. They'd fallen on Lily and it seemed to knock the wind out of her. But she pulled herself to the wall, away from the continuing scuffle. Before she could look up, she heard some sort of resounding, mechanical-*click*. She could only see the sneering Devil winking at her from Vic's back, as he seemed to be punching her brother on the floor.

There was a gasp. And suddenly Vic was still. A deathly silence draped over the room. When she moved against the wall, she could see Vic was looking down at her brother; he was sprawled out by the bed, his hands and fingers desperately intertwined over his stomach, his head cocked-up and peering down so that he had a double-chin.

There was blood dripping from the blade in Vic's hand. Hop-Along's blood. A strange twist of abnormal emotion went over Vic's face. He appeared both repentant and broken, he couldn't stop looking from the wet knife in his hand to the gushing belly of a kid who'd earned his name from following *him* around. The same kid he'd taught how to steal beer and bust into parking-meters.

Through the panting and the gasping, Hop-Along finally managed to speak, though it came out in whispers: "*...you're crazy, Vic ... I didn't ... didn't know ... how crazy ... didn't know...*" After that his head lolled back and thudded against the carpet, and Lily let out the most shrill, agonizing cry of terror and despair Vic had ever heard. He watched her run barefooted out of the room, and could still hear her screams as she went out of the apartment, down the stairs, out the front door, and (thanks to an open window) into the street.

"Jesus, Hop..." Vic was bent down, beside the body. He thought of closing Hop-Along's eyes for him, but he couldn't bring himself to touch him. Not again.

Soon he left the apartment, being sure to pick the gun back up on the way. All the neighbors were out and wondering what that racket was. Vic didn't give any replies. Only kept-on down the stairs, fishing for a smoke. He found his pack had been crushed in the fight. *Jesus Hop.* Outside the air was cold. The moon hung above Smokey Joe Mountain, clouds passing over. As with the night before, the fog was clearing.

And then he noticed something peculiar. Across the street, on the other side of a chain-link fence, trying to slide into his car, was Steady Jack. He'd forgotten Jack was supposed to meet him, but why was he over there? And why was he trying so hard not to be seen? Vic darted across the street to see.

Jack knew he'd been spotted and smiled as Vic approached, but didn't move from the open door. "Vic, I was just coming up to—"

Vic could hear the sirens. Squealing the way they do when in a hurry. Vic knew what was wrong when Jack's smile waned and he didn't seem shocked by the sudden sound. And when he rushed for the car. Vic grabbed him by the jacket and threw him to the concrete. Suddenly there was a pistol in Jacks face, and he was certain the guy with the crazy eyes holding it was going to shoot. "Why? *Why?*"

"Vic, I don't know what – "Jack was stuttering, he'd never stuttered before. Vic put the gun in his mouth and could still hear him stuttering. The sirens were almost there.

"Last chance, Jack." He took the gun out of his mouth.

Jack nodded his head, relenting. "The kid in the hospital ... he finally died. Cops already shut the

135

clubhouse down. We took a vote. All of us. We can't let you bring the heat down like this."

"So you dimed me out, huh?" Vic kept the gun aimed ahead, but he was grinning. He seemed ... happy. "Head Devil." He scoffed. "Well, guess what Jack? Believe it or not it's my lucky day. Let's got for a ride, Jack. I'll drive."

~ ~ ~

He was speeding up the mountain. He almost hadn't realized where he was, but when he did he became exultant. He stuck the .45 out the window, and let off round, after round, until the gun was empty, knowing that it would lead the last few squad cars that weren't already on him, his way. The Ford handled better than he could have ever dreamed of. Jack never deserved this ride. He was probably pissing all over the seats in the back. He was screaming as loud as Lily had and was moving restlessly about the car, looking for the first opportunity to tuck-and-roll safely; Vic made sure there were no chances for that.

The procession of pursuing police grew, the sirens drowning all other noise out (except Jack's cries). Vic cranked up the radio, laughing manically. This time he wasn't hearing the instrumentals of Link Wray.

"*...Well, the last thing I remember, Doc, I started to swerve ... and then I saw the Jag slide into the curve ... I know I'll never forget that horrible sight ... I guess I found out for myself that everyone was right ... WON'T COME BACK FROM DEAD MAN'S CURVE...*"

"How about that?" he called to Unsteady Jack in the back. "What're the chances of that Jan and Dean tune playing?"

"What the hell are you talking about?" Jack cried out. "It's a goddamn cola commercial!" The car skidded off the road then, just the slightest. It might not have been so bad if there'd been a railing of some sort to keep them from tumbling off the cliff. Vic just managed to keep them from plummeting over. The cops were skillfully keeping-up at each wild turn.

Suddenly the road seemed to dip back downhill, and at the end, seemed to disappear. They were at Dead Man's Curve. They both knew where they were, and as Jack broke into another high-pitched cry Vic stomped the gas-pedal until it was against the floorboard. He saw in the rearview that a few smart cops had dropped off, but the ones on his ass stayed. They were going to follow him *all the way.*

In the last few seconds, Vic shouted out, "Hey, Steady Jack! Ya ever see Pickens ride the bomb in Strangelove?"

Jack: *"HOLY SHIT!"*

WON'T COME BACK FROM DEAD MAN'S CURVE!

Vic: *"YAAA-HOOOOOO!"*

V

The Briefcase

1

"**D**on't Bogart that thing," Ricky Blantt said to his friend, Billy Joe, as the "Country Joe" song ended on the radio in Ricky's rusty green 63 Chevy pick-up. Billy Joe smirked, and passed over the joint that Ricky had laced with cocaine. His name wasn't really Billy Joe. Everyone else in town called him Bobby. But Ricky had been calling him Billy Joe since before they were old enough to drop out of high school. That's where they'd first met, and they'd been drinking buddies since. They sat in the same old truck, on the same long, isolated dirt road that ended at the top of the same hill they so often frequented, and drank Pabts Blue Ribbon, and had the same repetitive, time-consuming conversations and debates they'd been having for years.

"You're crazy! The Packers are better'n The Colts. They always have been, it's just a fact," said Ricky.

"No, they ain't," Billy Joe responded, holding the harsh smoke in his lungs.

"Don Majkowski is the best quarterback out there."

Billy Joe was exhaling when Ricky said this, and when he began laughing in amusement at the ludicrous statement his friend had made it sent him into a coughing fit. "What? The best?" he fought to say, still coughing into his balled-up fist. "Really? He might be good, but the best? What about Joe Montana? Dan Marino?"

"No, none of 'em. That Polack is the future of the NFL," Ricky insisted, flipping through the radio and cracking open a fresh beer.

"I'm almost f'sure that they lost to the Niners just a couple'a weeks ago."

"Nah, I don't think so." Ricky said, handing the smoldering joint back to Billy Joe. He *did* know that the Packers had lost to the Forty-Niners, but he didn't want to talk about it. Ricky stopped messing with the radio and left it on the channel he had originally strayed from. The music wasn't very loud and so they could hear the somnolent notes of the crickets chirping in the surrounding woods. It was about 10:30 p.m. and they had been parked in the same spot, drinking, for at least an hour. Billy Joe inhaled the thick smoke, deeply. He was always happy when Ricky had something they could smoke, or snort; you know, something to would go with the countless beers they would consume.

Billy Joe released the smoke from his lungs and out of the cracked window, into the night. "That some good blow, man. I can taste it more'n I can the grass. Who'd ya score it from?"

"Big Devan," Ricky answered, sipping his warm beer.

"Big Devan? You mean, Devan Tranch?" Billy Joe asked.

"Yea. Big Devan."

"Guess ya paid him back then, huh?"

"Nope."

When Ricky said this, Billy Joe was trying to ash the joint out the window but was so confounded by Ricky's answer that he smashed it against the glass when he spun his head around to look at him, smearing ashes all over his jeans and the floor of the truck.

"*Ay, watch it!*" Ricky lashed out.

"How the hell'd ya get it from him if ya ain't paid him the money ya already owe him?"

"What's it matter to ya?" Ricky asked sourly.

"It matters to you, man! Ya remember what he did to that kid, Davey?"

"Davey ... Davey..." Ricky repeated to himself, thinking. "Yea. Stutters sometimes, right?"

"He ain't gone be stutterin' anytime soon."

Billy Joe's laconic comment struck Ricky with a bit of interest, and he asked "What'a ya mean?"

"Tranch had that big, bald goon of his break the kid's jaw. Not to mention both his legs."

"Jesus jumpin' Christ, both of em? What in the hell'd Davey do?"

"Same thing you're doin'," Billy Joe replied. "Cept lil' Davey owed him a grand. So, there's that."

Billy Joe noticed the perturbed expression on Ricky's face as he was reaching for another beer.

"What? What do ya owe him? Fuck Ricky! You don't owe him more'n that do ya?"

As Ricky gazed out the window and into the black wilderness that encircled them, his mouth moved soundlessly up and down, exposing his bottom row of yellowed teeth; as if he couldn't remember how to speak, or just didn't want to. And just as the words began to slip past his tongue and into the world of articulation they both heard the abrupt sound of gunfire. They knew the explosions they were hearing were gunshots; along with everyone else who lived on the rural skirts of town, they were perfectly familiar with the sound. They fixed their eyes on the woods to the right of them, where they thought it was coming from. The shots sounded close, but they couldn't see anything. No flashes, no smoke. But the shots continued. Five, six, seven of them. "God what the hell is..." Eight, nine.

And then utter silence.

143

No more gunshots, no more crickets singing, even Ricky had turned his radio off when the shooting started seconds ago.

"What do ya think that was all about?" Billy Joe asked without taking his eyes from the woods.

"It was prolly just Skinny catchin' himself another buck in his yard."

"That wasn't Skinny's gauge. That sounded like pistols; different ones too," said Billy Joe, glaring into the woods.

"What, ya don't think his got any of those? He's prolly down there right now with one in each hand like Billy the Kid," Ricky said, opening his door to add another crumpled beer can to the small pile gaining stature on the road.

"Yea. Yea, your prolly right. So?"

"So, what?"

"You were sayin' what you owe Tranch?"

"Are you still houndin' me bout that? Christ, you're worse than my mother, Billy Joe. And give me that damn thing!" Ricky ordered, plucking the joint from Billy Joe's fingers. He took a deep drag from the cocaine packed roach and turned the radio back on.

2

They sat around another thirty minutes or so before heading back down the hill to continue their binge at Ricky's place. They were hesitant of pulling out of the woods and back onto the main road, because there was a chance that Sheriff Dowley would be out there sticking his snout around. Everyone in town was pretty much used to the almost routine shotgun blast that would come from Pete "Skinny" O 'Bryans property whenever a deer (or any other critter) was unfortunate enough to cross his lawn. But still, on occasions, Dowley would ride around, trying to reassure them all that he was there to stop any lawbreaking.

"Alright, alright. Tina Louise from Gilligan's Island or Elizabeth Montgomery from Bewitched?" asked Billy Joe, searching for some cigarettes in Ricky's glove compartment.

"Oh man," Ricky said, with sincere difficulty in his voice as he steered the pickup along the bumpy dirt road. "Can Elizabeth Montgomery grant me wishes?"

"I'm talkin' about Samantha from Bewitched, not Jeannie."

"Yea, but can she do magic for me an shit?" Ricky asked.

"Uhhh ... no. The actress, not her character."

"Tina Louise."

"Yea, me too," Billy Joe said, pulling out a pack of Marlboro Reds that were hidden in between several different maps. They were at the bottom of the hill now and making their way around the long, right hand curve that would bring them closer to the road that led to town.

"Ok, I got a good one," Billy Joe proclaimed. "Mamie Van Doran or Raquel Welch?"

"Oh, my god!" Ricky said, overwhelmed by his choices, still turning the truck right. Billy Joe chuckled a little to himself, he knew Ricky was particularly fond of both women.

"How could ya ask me somethin' like that? That's the toughest question I've ever..." Ricky's voice became feeble, and then the words trailed off altogether. They had reached the end of the long curve on the dirt road, and what was there in the middle, had not been there when they drove through an hour and a half ago.

3

They could see the body. It was just off to the left of the dirt road, where the grass started. They couldn't see the face, but the black dress shoes shined in the headlights of Ricky's truck. There was a white van off to the right of the road; it wasn't running. At first, neither Ricky or Billy Joe said anything, they both just stared. It would have been totally quite if it weren't for the steady purring of the trucks engine and the southern fellow singing a sad song on the radio inside of it. Billy Joe slowly took the cigarette out of his mouth and muttered, "What ... the ... fuck..." At least ten, long seconds passed before he spoke again, this time a little louder:

"Should we keep on goin'?"

"No. No, come on let's check it out," said Ricky, stepping out of the truck. Billy Joe put the cigarette back in his mouth and followed. Ricky was ahead, but they were both lumbering along, not too eagerly. Ricky was approaching the sprawled-out body just ahead of him, but his attention was diverted by the two that he noticed on his right once on the other side of the van.

"Holy shit!" Billy Joe cried out, thrown off his already wavering composure by this new discovery. They looked like bikers. Leather jackets and blue jeans, "What ... What'a ya think happened?" he asked.

Ricky moved a little closer and saw the gleam of a revolver in the grass by the dead biker closest to the van. "Looks like they shot each other," he responded.

Billy Joe had gone over on the other side of the road to look at the man in the polished dress shoes, when he shouted, "Ay, come look over here, Ricky!"

Ricky left the two unfortunates by the van and went over and stood next to Billy Joe. He saw a pale man with hair as dark and shiny as the shoes he was wearing, dressed in a black suit with a paisley tie. His pressed, white shirt was now mostly grisly crimson and had two large holes in it – at least two. His dark, empty eyes were still open, and a tough, haunting expression marred his face; his eyebrows arched at a sharp-angle of eternal fury. A .45 automatic was in his hand, his finger still on the trigger.

"Jesus," mumbled Ricky staring down, fixatedly. "Think he's from New York?"

"New York?" Billy Joe repeated stupidly, "what the hell would'e be doin' down here?"

"Well he ain't from round here, that's f'sure."

"Who knows where he came from. Don't matter now no ways," Billy Joe said. Then there was a muteness between them as they peered down at the well-dressed, nameless deadman. They could hear the same Creedence Clearwater Revival song that had been playing in cycle on the radio throughout the night; John Fogerty's voice echoed from Ricky's Chevy: **"Tombstone shadow ... stretchin' across my path ... Ev'ry time I get some good news, ooh there's a shadow on my back..."**

"What're we gonna do?"

"Not a goddamn thing! This ain't none of our business." Ricky said sternly.

"Sounds good to me," said Billy Joe, already heading back towards the truck. "Let's get on."

"Hold up!" Ricky said in a tone that forced Billy Joe to halt in nervous curiosity.

"What?"

"There's ... there's somethin' under him."

"Huh? What're ya talkin' about?"

148

"Looks like ... Looks like a suitcase, or briefcase or somthin'," Ricky dubiously stated.

"Now, why in the hell would there be a briefcase underneath him?"

"I don't know. Musta fell on top of it when he ... you know..." Ricky muttered, engrossed by what he'd found.

"Ok. So, there's a briefcase underneath him," Billy Joe said, visibly perturbed. He was eager to leave and get as far away from this... scene, as he could.

Ricky was on his hands and knees, trying to better inspect the briefcase that was lodged under the dead man. His eyes moved slowly as he peered up at Billy Joe with a crooked smile on his face and said, "Lets open it!"

"Open it?" Billy Joe asked incredulously. "What for?"

"Well, there must be somthin' sweet as sugar in there if these fellas were willin' to shoot each other up over it!"

"Nah, I don't think so."

"An why the hell not, Billy Joe?"

"Look over there!" Billy Joe insisted, "You ain't gotta be a tracker to see that another car parked over there got outta here in a hurry."

Ricky spun his head around and saw the brown furrows in an otherwise green patch of the shoulder. The tire tracks were deep and had torn out a sizeable amount of grass next to the road. Ricky had noticed it before, even in the dark, but hadn't considered mentioning it.

"Dead men don't drive," Billy Joe proclaimed. "If there was anything here worth somthin', whoever survived this musta made off with it."

Ricky took off his cap and ran his gauntly fingers through his thin brown hair once and said, "Well hell, there ain't no harm in lookin' is there?"

"Help..." the presumably dead biker farthest from the van groaned silently.

"Look all ya want and then let's get the heck outta here. I'm tellin' ya though..."

"Help ... Hel..." moaned the inflicted man, except this time coughing enough blood out into the air for the two ne'er do wellers arguing on the other side of the road to notice. Ricky shot to his feet and Billy Joe stumbled back next to him. "Holy shit!" he blurted.

"...Help..."

"Holy shit, he's still alive..."

4

They were standing over the stranger, looking down at him. Blood clotted his scruffy face and the bandana wrapped around his head. There was a tiny hole on the left side of his chest, just visible through the tear in the Rolling Stones shirt he was wearing. He would blink ever few seconds, but his eyes stayed mostly closed as his mouth moved up and down and his head turned from side to side. So far, there was a select word that seemed capable of fighting its way out of the stranger's mouth.

"Holy God," Billy Joe mumbled.

"Help..." The man managed to audibly whisper, spilling more blood from the corners of his mouth.

"What'a we do now?" Billy Joe asked with a shaky voice, unable to look away.

"What the fuck do ya mean?" Ricky snapped back. His eyes moved from Billy Joe back down to the bleeding stranger. "Let's get outta here."

"Ricky, we thought everyone was dead," Billy Joe reminded him, with the tone of someone who was feeling obligated.

"Shit, he's about to be. Look at him!"

"Ya ever hear of Karma, man?" Billy Joe asked, "We can't just leave the guy here like this."

"Oh, get the fuck outta here with that, Billy Joe! What the hell you ever done for anyone?" Ricky spat back, a little baffled at what his friend had just said. Billy Joe didn't say anything. He just stared at Ricky with a look that quite honestly made him want to laugh. Billy Joe's left eyelid was drooping lower than the right, and he was swaying a little in place. His face was that of drunk, vacuous redneck that didn't really have anything better to do.

"...Help..."

Ricky looked back and forth, between his suddenly good Samaritan of a friend, and the dying man, a few times before finally shouting, "Son of a bitch! Alright, fine. But we ain't goin' in, we're just gone drop him off in front of the hospital."

"You're such a softie," Billy Joe said, teasing him.

"Yea, whatever. He ain't gone make it to the hospital, and we're gone end up drivin' round with a dead outlaw in the bed of my truck ... Grab his head."

They scooped the stranger up and carried him over to the back of the Chevy and dropped him into its bed. Neither thought to see if there was a gun laying in the grass around the man.

5

When Ricky slammed the bed-door shut the stranger's eyes opened just enough to look at them. It was much too dark behind the truck to see the color of them. His mouth was moving, and the words still refused to come without a fight. But he was nodding his head up and down, slowly now. As if saying: "Thanks."

"Alright, let's get this done with," Ricky said, walking around to the driver's side. He got one foot through the door before remembering something. "Hold up, now. We almost forgot the case!"

"Ah Jesus, Ricky, come on. We gotta go before that fella bleeds to death in the back of your truck."

"He's already leakin' back there. I'll just hose it out later."

"Hell Ricky! I meant the part bout him dyin', not the inconvenience of you havin' to wash your dirty truck out!"

"It ain't gone take but a second, Billy Joe." And with that Ricky stepped away and headed back towards the body, not sticking around for further debate. Billy Joe sighed, but then hopped down from the passenger's seat and followed. Ricky bent down to the same spot as before. He could just see the handle of the briefcase, jutting out from beneath the dead man's arm. It was just enough to grab. He wrapped his fingers around it, then took hold from the bottom, and began to pull it towards him, warily. He kept his eyes on the dead gangster the whole time he slid the case in his direction. He stared at the corpse like it was a guard dog; as if any moment the man would wake up and fill him full of holes for trying to take the unknown treasure from him. The dark, leather outerwear of the briefcase squeaked and squirmed between the silky fabric of the man's suit and the earth below as it was freed from the crevice that held it.

Then it was free.

A plain, old Attache briefcase. With a lock. Billy Joe bent down next to Ricky for better perspective. Then he pointed at the lock and said, "Well, now what? You don't know the combination, do ya?" Ricky could hear him talking, but he wasn't listening. He reached out with both hands and pushed both latches opposite each other. There was a **click** and then it was open. Ricky and Billy Joe's eyes met simultaneously. What they saw in that briefcase was exactly what Ricky had been hoping for. All his life.

Money.

6

"Holy God. Would you just look at that? Is that a beautiful sight or is that a beautiful sight?" said Ricky, suddenly feeling chipper. Billy Joe stood next to him giggling like a child.

"Ah man," he said, "ah man, I'm lookin'."

Ricky began to titter with him. The briefcase contained two rows of twenty-dollar bills, six in each row. It was a large case, and it had to be just as deep inside. They couldn't begin to imagine how much money might be inside.

"Ah man, we're rich. We're fuckin' rich!"

"An you didn't even wanna check," Ricky reminded him with the slightest bit of condescension in his voice.

"You were right man, I can't believe it. It's amazin'! I'm apt to callin' it a miracle! Who would'a thought we'd be so lucky. I mean a row of cash for each of us!"

Ricky said nothing.

"You ain't gonna have to have n'worries, an I ain't gone have to worry bout goin' back to workin' in some stinkin' mill no more!" Billy Joe hailed triumphantly.

Ricky had a solemn expression on his face, like that of a man who had just discovered his winning lottery ticket was really a dud. He turned to him and said blandly, "Give me one of them cowboy killers, Billy Joe."

"Huh?" Billy Joe was takin' back a little by Ricky's look of misfortune. "Oh yea," he said, going through his jean pockets, then his flannel, finding the cigarettes from the glove compartment. He handed the pack over to Ricky and lit it for him.

"I mean, look at that! Easy livin' from now on brother. What should we..." Billy Joe finally shut up when he realized what Ricky was staring at with that steely look in his eye. He could hear a cough coming from the truck.

"Ah geez, I almost forgot all about the poor fella."

"I didn't." Ricky said with the fiery glow of a cigarette moving up and down in his lips.

"Well, I guess we'd better hurry on up then, huh?"

Ricky's eyes shifted quickly from the truck to Billy Joe's without blinking. Smoke poured out from his nose and mouth like steam from a kettle.

"What?" Billy Joe asked.

No response.

Again, he asked, "What?"

Ricky took another long, time-consuming drag of his cigarette and said flatly: "We can't take him to no hospital."

"What? What're ya talkin' about?" Billy Joe asked in honest ignorance.

"This changes things Billy Joe."

"How? What're ya talkin' about Ricky?"

"We can't take him. That's what I'm talkin' about."

"So, what? What, ya wanna just leave him here now?"

"Grow up, Billy Joe," Ricky said. "He's gone die anyway! 'Cept now his seen our faces. Heard us talkin', callin' each other by name. Hell, he even knows what the back of my truck looks like now."

"You were gone take him a second ago. What'd we put'm in the back for then?"

"Use that brain of yours, would ya? If we take him to a hospital he's gone live just long enough to tell the cops all about whatever happened here. Then all about the friendly fellas that were nice enough to take him there and then leave him bleedin' at the front door."

Billy Joe didn't know how to respond. He thought about what Ricky had just said. He thought about the stranger bleeding in the bed of the truck behind him. Then he thought about that briefcase. He'd had his eyes on the top row. He figured it didn't really matter what row he got, but his eyes had been set on the top since Ricky had popped the thing open. "I guess he is in pretty bad shape, huh?" he said, eyes still enchanted by the top row of twenties, rubber banded snugly, one next to another.

"He'd either die before we got there or make it long enough to throw us down the river," Ricky said, handing over his cigarette.

Billy Joe took it, inhaled the smoke, and nodded his head. "Yea. Yea, you're right," he said, revelation rising in his voice. "We can't help him without screwin' ourselves. Guess we shouldn't'a tried to get involved, huh?"

"You're too good-hearted Billy Joe, there ain't nothin' ya could'a done for him."

Billy Joe took another puff of the Marlboro Ricky had passed him. "Alright, well, guess it's best we put him back then, huh?"

Once again, Ricky didn't respond.

"What?" Billy Joe asked, uneasily. Ricky took his cigarette back and smoked it.

"Ah fuck, Ricky! What now, huh?"

Ricky exhaled the smoke from his last drag, before flicking the butt away and looking to Billy Joe and saying: "Can't leave him here, neither."

7

"Ya wanna kill him? Billy Joe blurted in astonishment.

"We can't just leave him here. What if someone comes by before he croaks and gets the cops? Or what if his biker buddies come lookin' for 'em? They gotta be waitin' for 'em somewhere. What if they come here an find 'em, and he tells 'em all about us? You really wanna bunch of greasy speed-heads ridin' round lookin' for ya?"

"Jesus, Ricky, this ain't the same thing as just leavin' an lettin' him take his chances."

"You said it yourself, it's him or us!"

"I didn't say nothin' like that!" Billy Joe shouted indignantly.

"You said we can't help him without screwin' ourselves. That's exactly what ya said," Ricky insisted.

"I said we couldn't help him, not, we couldn't leave his ass here!"

"It's the same conclusion can't ya see that, Billy Joe? If we leave him here, we gamble with **our** safety. We take a chance with **our** clean getaway. Ya wanna risk both of our asses for someone who's gone die no matter what. An *FUCK* Billy Joe, we'd be doin' him a favor! You really wanna leave him here to choke on his own blood? That's barbaric. Hell, the cows over at Daryl's slaughterhouse get it better'n that."

Billy Joe sat down on the grass, and without realizing it, started to rip handfuls of it from the ground. "I don't know Ricky..." he muttered, almost to himself. "...I don't know if I can..." Ricky peered down at his friend, who he thought resembled a frightened child at the supermarket who had lost his mother and was waiting for help to arrive. He took a deep breath and knelt, so he could be eye to eye. "I'm gonna ... I'm gonna level with ya, Billy Joe," Ricky said gravely. "I'm in trouble."

Billy Joe stopped tearing at the grass and looked to his friend. "What'a ya mean, trouble?"

Ricky spat off to his right, then rubbed his high forehead like a man who could take all the aspirin in the world and still have a headache. "You were askin' me earlier what I owe Devan Tranch ... Well ... I owe him a lot."

"How much?" asked Billy Joe.

"A lot more than he busted lil' Davey up for," Ricky told him, with his eyes on the dirt. He looked ashamed.

"God, Ricky. Why didn't ya say somethin'?"

"I don't know! I thought I could stall em ... I gave em half a grand last week to buy some more time. But now I just owe him interest too. Any day now, he'll be knockin' on my door with that animal who works for him, ready to break my neck when I tell em I ain't got it."

"Ricky ... I ... I..."

"What I'm sayin' is ... I'm in a bad spot no matter what we do, Billy Joe. My only chance outta this spot is in that there briefcase." The whole-time Ricky spoke, Billy Joe's eyes were on the top row of twenties in the briefcase. "I'm askin' ya ... No ... I'm beggin' ya ... I really need your help. You're my closest friend an I can't do it without ya, man." Ricky finished with what looked like tears beginning to manifest in his eyes. Billy Joe noticed this and didn't like it. Though he'd never admit it, even to himself, he thought of Ricky as the tougher of the two. He knew he needed to help Ricky, just as much as he needed the money for himself. He put a hand on Ricky's shoulder and said, "I'm here for ya brother. We've always looked out for each other."

Ricky gave his crooked smile. "Thanks, you're a good friend Billy Joe. I ain't gonna forget it."

They helped each other up, and then headed towards the truck. They got around to the back and saw that the stranger wasn't moving. "Guess we talked about it all too long. Fella finally let go."

Ricky didn't think so. He leaned a little closer and could see the sticky substance he knew was blood, shining faintly in the moonlight as the man's chest slowly heaved up and then back down. "Nah," he said, "he ain't dead, look at his chest movin'. He musta just passed out; lucky for him."

"What'a ya wanna do? Guess there should be some bullets in one of them guns."

"No. No, I gotta idea ... You still got that dirty ol' pile'a cinder blocks in ya backyard, by your ol' Chevy?"

"Yea..." Billy Joe answered curiously. "Why? What're ya thinkin'?"

"I'll tell ya 'bout it on the way. We gotta stop by your place first. Get at least two of them blocks."

Billy Joe just stared at him with his mouth ajar. A bit of a comical, puzzled expression on his face. "Never mind 'bout it right now!" Ricky spat out, seeing Billy Joe's confused hesitation. "Just get in the truck. I'll get the case."

8

Ricky went over and kneeled in front of the briefcase that was still open next to the dead stranger. The crooked smile now stretched to both sides of his face. He let out a snicker to himself as he eyed every inch of the money, at least the money he could see on top. He shut the case, taking a mental note that the combination shown when he opened it was 333, just in case. Then jogged over to the truck that still had swamp rock n roll echoing out of its open doors into the otherwise silent night and an unconscious bleeding criminal/witness in the bed of it. He didn't count any of the money, or even touch it.

9

It was just after midnight when they pulled onto the Deep River Memorial Bridge that resided on the heels of the county. The crepitating creaking the old truck caused as it rolled over each corroding plank of wood on the truss bridge seemed thunderous in the still of the dreary night. Ricky slowed when they reached the center of the bridge, then put the truck into park. Billy Joe looked around with a renewed look of confusion. Ricky hadn't told him where they were going or what they were going to do, but when they stopped in the middle of the dark, lonesome bridge with the innately roaring tides of the Kenduskee River flowing beneath them – and straight into the next three counties – he got the idea.

"You wanna? ... Jesus Ricky, that's *sick!*" Billy Joe said, rubbing his stomach in some attempt at placating this new feeling of anxious sickness.

"Take it easy, he's passed out remember," Ricky reassured him in a voice of commiseration.

Billy Joe let out a huge breath and then began rubbing his hands together after giving up on his stomach pains. Ricky sized him up for a moment, and then said with a pat on the back, "Come on buddy, don't fall apart on me now. We're almost to easy livin', huh?"

"Yea ... yea..." he said, nodding to Ricky. And Ricky nodded back, then he hopped out of the truck and onto the bridge that they both knew well; they ought to, it'd been there since before either of them were born. And since they'd been born, they'd been to the spot more than once for 'misdemeanorish purposes.' Billy Joe got out, and they made their way towards the back. Each step they took echoed in the night. The night's fog was dense, and the only real source of light was coming from the old truck. Ricky got around to the back first and dropped the bed door, fast, out of pure instinct, and found the man lying next to it. And awake.

10

Billy Joe came from the other side of the truck and saw this. "Ah fuck, Ricky!" he shouted. They were both staring down at the stranger, but they each had a very different look on their faces.

"Plea ... Pleas..." The dying man's words were hardly intelligible. He was frailly coughing blood out onto his chin and down his shirt each time he tried speaking.

"It's alright. It don't change nothin'."

Billy Joe spun his head around to Ricky. "What the hell ya mean it don't change nothin'? He's awake, that changes a lot!"

"Plea ... Ple..."

"It don't change nothin' Billy Joe," Ricky said, now looking at him. "He's so out of it, he ain't gone know what's happenin'."

"No, no I can't do that, Ricky. This whole thing is fucked up, but this is just too much."

"Would you quit bein' such'a woman bout all this! We're at the finish line, Billy Joe!"

They were too busy arguing to notice the man bleeding on the door of the truck next to them, was using all of his strength to get his hand to the inside of his leather jacket.

"Is this really worth it?" Billy Joe asked, his voice trembling. "Look where we are! Think about what we're doin' here!"

"Did you forget everything I told ya 'bout back there? Did you forget the *shit* that I'm in? Your're more worried for a fella ya don't even know than ya are 'bout ya best friend!"

The bleeding stranger lying next to them, just a couple feet below, was doing his best to get the long barrel .44 magnum all the way out of his jacket.

"We can still take the money. We just ain't gotta drown this poor bastard!"

"We've been over this, Billy Joe! This is the only way we can be sure we're in the clear! Ya makin' it sound like I wanna do this. I don't wanna do this! I–" The man's revolver was out of his jacket, and he was using everything he had left in him to lift it up and put Ricky in his sights. "–so, sack up, would ya!" Ricky finished.

"It's wrong Ricky! It's just all wrong!"

"Ya wanna know what's wrong? I'll tell ya what's wrong! This godda ... *OH SHIT!*" Ricky cut off when he finally glanced down and noticed the business-end of the magnums barrel pointed right at his gut; which seemed to be as high as the man could lift it. He was squeezing the trigger ... or trying to, anyway. But he had lost too much blood and was so feeble and exhausted that he couldn't seem to muster the strength he needed to squeeze the trigger just tight enough. He just couldn't seem to apply the last bit of modest pressure needed to drop the gun's hammer; which Ricky could see moving back and forth at the same time the cylinder spun slowly right to left, then back from left to right, one empty chamber dancing with a live one as the stranger tried to fire point blank into Ricky's stomach.

With one swoop, Ricky snatched the gun from the man's hand. "*PHHHEEEEWWWWW* ... Holy shit ... Holy shit..." Ricky babbled. He was completely baffled that this incapacitated stranger, who had been bleeding in the back of his truck for almost an hour, had nearly blown him away with this *fucking hand-cannon*. He put his free hand on his chest and could feel his heart pulsating wildly. It made him think of the scene in that space movie where John Hurt's chest bursts open. And that sent another wave of ball-tightening terror through him.

"Jesus, where the hell'd he get that from?" an almost equally bewildered Billy Joe asked.

"Musta had it on him," Ricky said timidly, without taking his eyes from the stranger; there was fearful realization in them. He knew just a second or two later, and this fella might've been able to squeeze off a shot.

"Please ... plea ..." the man whispered, still too weak to speak vibrantly, let alone fire a gun.

Ricky took a few slow steps back, unable to remove his gaze from the man lying on the bed door of his truck, quietly pleading through the blood that he was gargling. Billy Joe noticed the rare look of fear in Ricky's eyes, and again, it made him uncomfortable. "Alright." He said, but Ricky didn't hear him. He went over and put his hand on Ricky's shoulder and said, "Ay Ricky, ya hear me? Come on, man, let's get this done, brother."

Ricky jumped, just the slightest, when Billy Joe's hand touched his shoulder, finally forcing his eyes from the stranger. But it snapped him back into reality. "Ok ... Ok," he said, nodding his head and putting his own hand onto his friend's shoulder." "Thanks, Billy Joe." He let go of him and walked over to the wooden railing of the bridge and looked down. He couldn't see a thing. There was only blackness. But he could hear that one-way roaring of the river that he knew was only twenty feet or so below him. He stretched his hand out, holding the large revolver that had just been pointed at his stomach, and dropped it into the unseen murky waters below. He thought he heard a splash, but he couldn't be sure.

11

"Get one of them cinder blocks," Ricky ordered Billy Joe, as he started zipping the stranger's jacket about a third of the way up. All the stranger could do was shake his head from left to right as Ricky tucked the man's jacket into his jeans, and then tightened the belt as much as he could.

"Just one?" Billy Joe asked, dropping a heavy eroding block onto the trucks bed door.

"Yea, I think one'll do it."

The man began to shake his head more desperately when Ricky placed the heavy concrete block onto his chest and started to ease the flaps of the jacket over it. Ricky could feel the man's hands grasping at his sleeve while he did this, but he brushed him off each time without paying any mind. He fit the brick on the man's chest inside of the jacket and then finished zipping it, this time all the way to the top.

"Don't ... Don't..." The stranger pleaded as loud as he could, but it came out in mere whispers.

"I got the top, you grab his feet," Ricky said with a kind of indifference to the order, that only minutes ago, before a strange man pointed a gun at his friend, would've made Billy Joe nervous.

They lifted the man off the door and teetered towards the same part of railing where Ricky had dropped the revolver. The pressure from the hefty block resting on his chest made the man cough out even more blood; most landed on his jacket, reacquainting with the coagulated blood that had been coughed out earlier. And some made a faint spotted trail, leading from the truck to the railing as they reached it.

Billy Joe looked down at the man's face once last time and saw that it was rife with panic and debility. His head still shook, and his bloody lips quivered as he muttered:

"...no ... no ... don't..."

And with that, Ricky and Billy Joe heaved the man up, onto, and then over the barrier. Quickly, they hung their heads over the post to see the stranger disappear into the black tributary below. He vanished into the shadows instantly. But this time, Ricky was sure that he heard a splash.

12

Twenty minutes later they were turning onto a dirt road hidden by the surrounding woods, not unlike the one where their eventful evening had begun; except this one lead to Ricky's home. They didn't speak the whole ride back, and even though the radio was on the whole time, neither would've been able to tell you what was playing. The crowded oaks began to dye down, and soon they were out of the woods all together and in the front yard of Ricky's secluded farmhouse. It was a one-story home and the red paint was wearing away all over. To the left of the house and in the back yard was a shed that once might have been used for storing tools, but in the last decade had only been used as another hangout for Ricky and Billy Joe to drink and bring (questionably) appropriately-aged party girls. It had the same eroding red paint to match the house beside it. Ricky navigated the loud, old pickup around the vast amount of junk that filled his yard. When he got closer to the house, he parked the truck by an old John Deer lawnmower that was missing all its wheels (and god only knew what else), and that was when he noticed the deadpan look on Billy Joe's face. He was staring straight out of the window at the ugly red house but wasn't really *seeing* the house. He appeared to be totally lost in thought, and Ricky wondered if he even knew where they were.

"Ay!" Ricky said, snapping his fingers in front of Billy Joe's face, which was enough to pull him out of whatever kind of trance he was in. "You wanna beer?"

"Ya know I do."

"Well that's good. Cause we got some celebratin' to do!" Ricky shouted gleefully, with his right hand resting on top of the briefcase that lay between them.

13

Ricky threw his keys down on the kitchen table, then with one arm swept several empty beer cans off the side of the table and into the overflown trash ben beside it. Several crumpled cans missed all together and fell to the floor; where they remained. Then he grabbed some mail and a Rifleman magazine from the table and tossed it over onto the counter by the microwave.

"Grab some beers would ya? Ya know where the fridge is, don't ya?" he asked while making room on the table, and then diligently placing the briefcase on top of it.

Billy Joe just smirked. Even if he hadn't been in this very kitchen hundreds of times, the fridge was right there beside Ricky, and right there in front of him. He grabbed four Pabts Blue Ribbons from an already opened twenty-four pack and tried to hand two of them to Ricky. But after he realized that Ricky was too busy preparing himself for the opening of the briefcase – or just plain ignoring his polite gesture – he put the beers down on the table and then cracked one of his open. He sipped at it, savoring the small amount of foam that came from the can, and then the actual beer itself; instead of chugging as much of it as he could on the first gulp, like he normally would. For some reason sipping his drink, rather than putting it away as fast as he could just to have another, just seemed more soothing to him at the moment.

CLICK

Ricky had popped the case open, and that crooked smile was back.

"Ho-ly– fuck. I'll never get tired of lookin' at that!" said a suddenly upbeat Billy Joe before he commenced to gulping down half the beer he had just been savoring. Ricky's hand moved inside of the case and onto the money. His hand began to gently glide across the bills, almost like he was caressing them. Then suddenly the smile on his face was gone.

"We should go on over to that strip joint, in Clayton. What'ya think?" asked Billy Joe.

Ricky didn't answer.

"Or ya wanna just stay in and get zooted?"

Ricky took his hand from the briefcase and closed it. "I gotta take a shit. Just hang out in here and drink my beer. And count the cash will ya?" he said, walking out of the kitchen and down the hall. Billy Joe noticed that he took the two beers from the table with him.

14

Billy Joe finished the last of his beer, crushed the can, then threw it half-heartedly at the packed trash ben. It fell to the floor, joining the rest of the clutter. He let out a sigh, then went over and picked it up. Realizing it had no place to fit in the mountainous pile of cans residing inside of the ben, even if he had placed it delicately on top. He set the crumpled can down on the table, beside the briefcase. He opened a second beer, and then flipped on the little 20-inch television set at the other end of the counter. But as soon as he saw David Letterman welcoming him to the show he flipped it back off. That was when he thought he heard a thud. A familiar thud, the thud of wooden door meeting wooden frame, that sounded like Ricky's backdoor.

"Ricky?" He shouted out into the hallway. There was no response. He waited and listened for a moment, then shrugged it off.

He went over to the cabinet above the microwave, opened it, and was disappointed to find nothing but Ramon noodles and off-brand Captain Crunch.

"He doesn't even have any milk," Billy Joe mumbled.

Then he started shuffling through the bread basket, looking for the oatmeal raisin bagels that Ricky typically kept around. He didn't find any, and he wasn't about to eat plain white bread.

If only Ricky had a toaster, he thought. *He'd better go on out an get one with his share.*

He took a sip of his beer and noticed that he'd almost finished it.

What the hell's takin him so damn long?

He glanced back over at the table and saw the Rifleman magazine. He picked it up and started flipping through the pages.

"Gun laws, gun laws, gun laws..." he muttered, closing the magazine and motioning to put it back from where he got it. But he didn't put it back.

He saw something that stopped him.

Something that the magazine in his hand had been covering. A stack of opened letters had been underneath The Rifleman's latest issue. Usually, Billy Joe wouldn't have paid them any mind. He would have kept drinking his friend's beer and waiting for him to return from his necessary human function. But the top letter, had something unexpected stamped across its cover. Two words in big bold letters.

FORECLOSURE NOTICE

He placed the magazine down to the side, along with his mostly empty beer and dug into the envelopes contents like it was his own. His lips moved in silence as his eyes skimmed from line to line. The message was a little prolonged and formal for Billy Joe, but he understood what mattered. This letter was saying that Ricky hadn't been keeping up with payments, on *anything*, and that he owed his bank money. A lot of money. And that one way or another, they were going to get it.

What kind of hole had his friend dug himself into? That was when he looked down at the other letters. The *second* foreclosure notice. He held it up next to the first in comparison. There were some noticeable differences in this one, so he read over it too. This letter was a bit more difficult for him to comprehend, but he got the idea that this one was another warning (another warning that cost interest, warnings always seem to cost interest, even banks charge fucking vig).

"Jesus..." He was so stunned by the letters in his hands, that he didn't even notice the others on the counter: electric bills, on top of water bills, on top truck repair bills, on top of student loan debts he'd managed to get from some sucker start-up company without proof of enrollment, on top of more bills.

Christ, what would he have done if we hadn't found the briefcase? Is that luck or what? Why didn't he tell me 'bout this? I could understand the Tranch thing, but fuck this is a whole other story.

And then he heard that thud again, and this time, he knew it was Ricky's backdoor. Hastily, he dropped both the notices where he found them, and then slid the Rifleman magazine back over them. He could hear the wooden boards of the hallway creaking as Ricky's work boots pressed against them with each step he took towards the kitchen. The last thing Billy Joe wanted was for Ricky to walk in on him, snooping through his private shit. He threw his head back and chugged down the rest of his beer as Ricky appeared in the doorway. Billy Joe belched, crushed the can, and then pretended that he only just noticed Ricky standing there, with his own beer in his hand.

"Goddamn, it took ya long enough. Were you drinkin' that on the shitter?"

Ricky looked down at the Pabts Blue in his hand like he hadn't known it was there. "I was thirsty," he replied.

"Ah, man, that's disgustin'. What'd ya squat in the lawn? I heard the door openin' an closin'."

"I was lookin' for somethin'. Come on, grab that case out the fridge an lets drink it in the crack shack."

15

The "crack shack," as Ricky had referred to, was the callow name he and Billy Joe shared for the dirty red tool shed in the backyard (though they had indulged inside of it plenty), and that's where they were heading.

"Did ya count the money?" Ricky asked, opening the same backdoor Billy Joe had just heard moments ago.

"Aw, goddamnit!" said Billy Joe. He hadn't counted the money inside of the briefcase. He'd forgotten all about it once he'd surreptitiously glanced over Ricky's secret mountain of debt.

"It's alright. It ain't goin' nowhere," said Ricky.

They were halfway across the lawn before Billy Joe had to say something.

It was killing him inside not to. Just like back in the ninth grade when he fucked Ricky's ex -girlfriend, Jessie. He'd only managed to keep that a secret for an hour or so, before calling Ricky to confess and apologize for something he'd had no idea about. He knew Ricky couldn't stay mad at him. He was always there to help him.

"Look bro, I gotta talk to ya about somethin'."

Ricky stopped and spun his head around and looked at his friend like he already knew what he was going to say. But he didn't.

"I ... I saw the letters. Ya know, them warnings. The ones from the bank on your counter."

There was silence between them again.

"Why didn't ya tell me about all this shit, man? How the hell did this even happen? It said they were gonna come for ya house if ya don't pay 'em?"

Ricky didn't say anything. He only looked back at the shed.

"Ricky!"

"Ah hell, Billy Joe!" He finally snapped back, "Why the hell would I tell ya? What're ya gonna do, huh? Win the lottery? Rob a Wells Fargo and then give me all the money?"

"This here briefcase changes things, man. It changes everything. Whatever happened to cause this shit don't matter. It's like a fucking gift from God!" Billy Joe attested.

"I know ... I know. It's just..."

"What?" Billy Joe asked in a less patient tone.

Then, with a harried tone, "What if it ain't enough?"

When Ricky said that, Billy Joe's impatient understanding turned into pity. This was his best friend, and he was in trouble. Some city slick with a comb-over and a dull suit was gonna come here and take away his home. And on top of that, Tranch was gonna get his pale ogre to smash his face in.

"Fuck, Ricky, after everything that happened tonight, ya know I ain't gonna let it end like this. If your half ain't enough ... I'll chip in some outta mine. We'll worry bout payin' me back later on down the road. We'll make sure these assholes don't come fuck with you first."

A non-crooked smile began to form on Ricky's face but didn't quit make it.

"You're a damn good friend, Billy Joe," he said, "I'm sorry bout everything that's happened here tonight. I know it's my fault, I just ... I don't know, it's like I can't help it..." He finished, going over and putting his hand on Billy Joes shoulder for the second time that night. "But I'll never forget everythin' ya done for me, buddy. Never."

Billy Joe did smile.

"Yea, yea, now get off me ya queer, and let's get torn up, huh?"

Ricky grinned out of the side of his mouth and let Billy Joe lead the way into the crack shack.

16

Billy Joe was still smiling when he opened the door to the shed and stepped inside. Even when he saw the garbage bags duct-taped all over the wall opposite him. In fact, he started laughing. He figured Ricky had gone and done something stupid during another drunken escapade and put a hole in the wall somehow. But what happened to the floor? There were bags taped on the floor below the wall as well. Billy Joe moved closer for inspection, still chuckling. Ricky was behind him, picking something up from behind the door.

"Now, what in the hell happened here?" Billy Joe asked, amused, "I don't think that'll stop the critters from gettin'..." When he turned around to look at Ricky he knew immediately what the garbage bags were for.

Ricky had a jittery look on his face, holding the double barrel shotgun. He hadn't wanted his friend to turn around and see what was coming. He was still pulling back the second hammer.

"RICKY NO!"

Both hammers fell, and Billy Joe's blood covered the room.

17

It was everywhere. In places, he hadn't even thought of, or imagined, it could be. Fuck, he didn't have enough garbage bags for this. The ones he had put up were only covered in bits of blood spatter, and the ones on the floor had only caught his friend after he'd fallen backwards. But it wasn't stopping the river of blood that was slithering from his friends mangled skull and onto the floor. It didn't seem to be slowing down either. He looked to the shallow ceiling above and saw the kind of mess he'd thought would've filled the plastic shields he'd taped up. Thick clumps of what had to be brain matter clung to the ceiling as blood dripped down like dew drops in a cave. Ricky started to back out of the shed before the blood coming from his pal's head could touch his boot. He felt nauseas. He could taste all the beer he'd drunk that night in tiny belches he let out in an attempt at some relief for his stomach. He dropped the shotgun in the grass and covered his mouth, hoping to stop the sick that he knew was coming. But then he felt something wet on his hand and he knew it was blood before even looking. And that was the end of trying to hold his beer down. He dropped to his knees and let it out. Twice.

When he finished, he managed to get his flannel off and wipe his face. Removing the combination of blood and vomit. He saw that and threw up some more. The coppery, penny-like smell of blood overpowered the smell of his sickness, and that only made it worse to him. He wanted to get away from it. But his legs wouldn't allow it.

The pool of blood that had consumed the floor of the crack shack was now spilling out, first onto the concrete block, used as the one and only step into the shed, and then down onto the few living blades of grass below it.

The discomfort in his stomach had subdued for the most part, but he still couldn't bring himself to stand.

Jesus. He thought, "*I'll never clean all that up tonight. Fuck. Alright, well ... First things first ... First things first...*

18

The bridge looked the same as it had just hours ago. If Ricky didn't know any better, he'd have sworn that the half-moon glaring indifferently from the sky was in the same place, lurking transparently behind the same, foreboding clouds billowing by. But things weren't the same. He was alone this time. And a body crudely duct-taped around a tarp with a cinder block inside of it is difficult to move on your own; Ricky had already considered this. He stopped the truck and threw her in reverse. Then he cranked the steering wheel left and backed the truck up against the banister. He went a little too fast and hit the railing. He didn't mind, he hardly noticed. There was far too much on his mind to be worried about the exterior beauty of his ol' pickup. He hopped out, stepped up onto the back wheel, and climbed into the bed of the truck with Billy Joe. He was pleased to see that the tapped-up tarp had kept anymore blood from spilling out.

It goddamn shoulda'. I used two whole rolls of duc tape on it. Shit, I can't hardly see any tarp through it.

He grabbed ahold from what he assumed were the legs and pulled towards the wooden rail that was only a few inches taller than the door of the truck. It was heavy. Very heavy.

Good thing I told him to grab two of them blocks.

He got it halfway over the railing and was able to push it off from there. He didn't lean over to look this time, but he heard the same splash as he had before, maybe louder. Definitely louder.

19

Ricky Blantt practically collapsed into the chair in his kitchen. The sun would be coming up soon, but there was no time for sleep. He had things to do. The briefcase was in the same place it'd been since being brought to his kitchen table. For a moment, he just stared at it. The discovery of this thing had altered his life completely within a night, and he still didn't know exactly how much money was in there. When he remembered that he got a little excited. How much could fit in that thing? Had to be a lot. He crushed his cigarette butt into the ashtray (a ripped in half beer can) and shot his hands to the latches of the case.

CLICK.

There it was. Exactly how he had found it and left it. What he'd worked so hard for. He could hardly contain himself, and in his excitement, he grabbed the first stack he could get to, on the top row. And his crooked smile disappeared.

Something was very wrong. Underneath the stack of money, was the corner of what looked like a Yellow Pages phone book.

Stark panic washed over him, and he swiped the rest of the money out of the way and saw only an encyclopedia and two Yellow Pages next to it. Even the visible stacks of money weren't quite what they seemed; beneath the twenty-dollar bills that lay on top, were mere cut out pieces of notebook paper.

NO, he thought. *NO! NO! NO! NO!*

*"Fuck! Fuck! Fuck! **FUCK!**"* He howled, flipping over the table in a rage.

"NO ... No, it can't. That don't make any Goddamn sense!" he babbled to himself pacing back and forth wildly. The first thought that crossed his mind was that Billy Joe must've done this while he was out in the shed, setting up the ... well, setting up. But that was making less and less sense. He didn't have any of those books lying around the house, and he knew that Billy Joe hadn't been just walking around with them down his pants. Then he remembered the horror show where they'd found the briefcase, and how it looked like the end of a Spaghetti Western. Everyone dead, gun in hand. And that made Ricky start to think, that maybe, just maybe, he'd found out why.

20

Two hours and most of the twenty-four pack later, Ricky was still in the chair. The table was back upright, but only so he could stack the empty beer cans on top of one another. The briefcase, and its unfortunately misleading contents, remained scattered on the floor. He rubbed out another cigarette butt in a now full ashtray and finished the beer in his hand. He tried to place it at the top of his aluminum pyramid, but it collapsed the moment he touched it. He went off cackling, wiping the backwash that had spilled in his lap. He laughed and laughed, looking at the mess around his kitchen. And then the laughter died out, slowly, and turned into the frown of a tired, lonely, and frightened man.

"...I'm sor ... sorry ... I'm sorr..."

Ricky buried his head into his arms that were crossed on the table and shut his eyes tightly.

21

Bang! Bang! Bang! Bang!

He woke up to the pounding at his front door. He was so startled (and still drunk) that he jumped and collapsed from his chair. He didn't stand back up; not yet. He just sat there, rubbing at his eyes and listening to the banging at his door.

Bang! Bang! Bang!

He knew it was Devan Tranch before Devan Tranch even spoke up.

"Ricky!" came the raspy, muffled voice of Tranch through the door. "Riiiiiicccccckkkyyyyy!"

Ricky pulled himself up from the floor, using the table for support.

What time is it? Don't matter I guess.

"RICKY!" The voice and the knock were getting louder, much less tolerant of an anticipated response. Ricky knew it wasn't Tranch knocking; it was the white hulk that worked for him, and he came to smash. He only had a ten-dollar bill in his wallet, and the two hundred and forty on the floor from the briefcase; that was less than half of what he'd paid him a couple weeks ago for more time. Hell, the interest he owed him was more than that!

"Ricky! Don't make us let ourselves in! You hear?"

Bang! Bang! Bang!

Ricky stood in his kitchen, listening to the two debt-collecting thugs beating at his door to get inside, and thought about his choices. The way he saw it, he had two of them: Open the front door and risk getting his neck broken, or take off through the back, run for it, and try to make it another day.

VI

Lunchroom Verdict

"So, what's it gonna be? The pasta dish from Manelli's' or Dominick's Subs?"

"Jesus Christ, Gorello! We're tryin' to fuckin' talk, here," Lorre chided from across the table. His sonorous voice was tough and gravelly from years of smoking those fat Corona cigars – like the one dangling out of his thin mouth now, fastened by clenched teeth that he managed to speak through with the unoccupied side of his mouth. His ornery demeanor was only emphasized by his shaggy eyebrows that seemed to rest at a perpetual sinister arch, coming together in a tight furrow just above his nose. Double-karat gold rings adorned most of the spatulate fingers he used to occasionally ash his cigar or pour another Cognac. "I thought your physician put you on a diet, anyway?"

"She did," Gorello replied, shrugging and blotting at the perspiration sousing his forehead with a damp handkerchief. He was a grossly stout man, with a pencil-thin mustache as dark and glossy as the hair on his head, who breathed heavily and always seemed to be saturating dark spots of sweat throughout his lavish tailored suits. "But what she don't know won't hurt her." He gave a lone titter and went back to the menus he'd been studying intently.

Lorre started again, "Now like I was sayin'–"

Gorello cut in once more, hollering out, "Trisha! Trish, get in here!"

"For fucks sake, Gorello! We ain't here for a goddamn thanksgiving feast, ya know! We got somthin' we need to talk ab–"

The door opened, and a lean, mature-looking woman attired in a garish cheetah-print blouse and a pair of tight-fitting slacks wandered into the stuffy room. From the gaping door, the resounding jukebox jives the girl's downstairs were dancing to came spilling into the room.

"You call, hon?" the woman asked, twirling a red lock of her hair with a long, acrylic-nailed finger.

"So, what's it gonna be?" Gorello asked the others around the table.

"I'd like a sub," said Costello, the youngest of the bunch.

Taro: "You always get the sub. You eat one of Dom's subs every day."

"Dom's subs are good," spoke Rossini for the first time in the meeting.

"I'm not sayin' they aren't. I'm sayin'—"

"*Beat it*, Trish," Lorre growled impatiently.

Gorello: "Now wait a minute, Eddie—"

"Beat it, I said," Lorre reiterated coldly.

She frowned and did as she was told; this wasn't the first time he'd spoken to her that way.

When she was gone Gorello spoke, "What'd you do that for, Lor? We're starvin' here."

"I'm tryin to talk about whether we should whack this fuckin' guy, and all you can think about is lunch! This is important, can you remember that? Or do you gotta wait outside while the big boys make the tough decisions?"

Gorello glowered and went back to his menus.

Lorre: "Anyone else?"

No one said anything.

"Alright," Lorre went on, "Now we all know Little Mickey Puraro got pinched in that raid last week. What we also might know ... is that he could've talked – or still might talk ..."

Costello spoke up, "I don't think he'd talk. Really."

Lorre almost looked displeased. "Yea? Well what if he does? That's the real question."

Taro: "I thought the question was whether he talked at all?"

"And I thought it was what we were doin' for lunch!" Gorello barked.

Costello went on, "Remember, this is a guy that did almost his whole dime-stretch for a hijacking job that he didn't even pull. If that isn't proof that he's no squealer then I don't know what is."

"Yea," Lorre said, "but that's exactly why he might talk now; they're gonna wanna put him away forever this time. Why wouldn't he talk?"

"I still don't think he'd sing."

"No one ever thinks they'll sing, but they almost always do."

"What if we're wrong?" Costello said.

Lorre shrugged blithefully, drawing from his cigar between sentences. "Then we're wrong. And we get another guy anyway."

"I know! I've got it!" Gorello proclaimed. "The pasta. Let's get the pasta! How about it?"

Taro: "Sounds good to me."

"We'll take a vote," said Lorre.

Gorello: "About the pasta?"

"No, not about the fuckin' pasta! About knockin' off Puraro!"

Rossini: "All for it?"

All but Costello and Gorello raised their hands; when Lorre cleared his throat Gorello peered back up from the menu and rose his own hand impassively.

"Ok," said Rossini, swaying patiently in his seat. "Let's have it, Costello."

"I just don't think we got enough to clip this guy. This whole thing is based on assumptions. He's got the past on his side, that ten years he did for -"

"Yea you mentioned that already," Lorre interjected crossly. "Are they gonna have to reopen The Rock and give ya your pick of the cells for you to get the picture? If we stick around and wait for it in writing, *it'll be too late!*"

"But all we have is the *IF*."

Lorre smooshed his cigar in frustration and leaned forward, his Cartier clinking against the crystal decanter of the Remy Martin he slid out of the way. "Yea, well it's a pretty substantial *IF*. Now look Costello, everyone is for it but you, so it's gonna happen anyway. The best thing you can do is to go along with it while you still can."

Lorre was glaring at him tempestuously, his eyes glinting with suppressed outrage. Costello realized the others were beginning to glare with him. "Ok," he submitted, "Ok."

"Good. Then it's a yes on the contract," Lorre rubbed his hands together before intertwining his fingers and resting the back of his head in his palms; a gesture of satisfaction.

"Well I'm glad we got *that* out of the way," said Gorello. Then he hollered for Trish again.

This time she only poked her head through the door. "You boys make up your minds?"

Gorello: "Yea, we're going with the pasta dish, ain't we?"

Lorre grunted indifferently.

Costello: "I don't know, I think I'd still prefer one 'a Dominick's subs."

Rossini: "Yea, I'm sort of thinking subs, too."

Gorello flung his hands in the air, "Jesus Christ! Why the hell wouldn't you say something?"

VII

When They Came Back

It was about 10:30 P.M. when the city cab pulled to the curb of a residence in the respectable downtown neighborhood of Five Points. A residence it had been to three times before this night. From the backseat, a tall, dark-haired man opens the door and steps out. His attire – pants, sports shirt, and trench coat – all black. The man took a final drag of the Lucky Strike he'd been smoking before shooting it into the street with his middle finger and thumb. The smoldering cherry rolled along the pavement to a halt, as the man ambled around to the back of the car. There was a click as the trunk was opened from inside the cab. The tall man took out the one, stuffed suitcase he'd brought with him on his "Business trip," and one duffle bag that he'd never seen before then.

But he knew that it would be in there. It always was.

He set the luggage down on the curb and leaned into the opened window of the passenger's side door. His left hand was fishing inside of his coat, and when he brought it back out he was holding a large, thick, rubber-banded stack of money.

"Tell 'em, as always, it's been a pleasure." He said, removing a one-hundred-dollar bill from within the stack and handing it over to the driver.

"As always, they feel the same," the driver responded in an impassive tone, taking the C-note and stuffing it into his own pocket. The man leaning in through the window gave a sinister grin that would've made a young Richard Widmark proud. "'Till' next time," he said backing away from the car.

"Until' next time." The driver agreed, shifting the car into drive.

The tall man stood by his luggage, both old and new, and watched as the cab pulled away. It drove down the dimly lit one-way street that lead back to Rosewood Ave, and then disappeared.

"Till' next time," he said again. Only this time to himself. Still grinning.

~ ~ ~

After setting his luggage down by the stairs, the man closed and locked the front door, then took off his coat and hung it on one of four hooks on the wall. He went over to the bar, that he'd had built just last summer, in between the kitchen and the living room. He examined the array of fine costly liquors and selected the Johnnie Walker blue. He grabbed a crystal glass and some ice, and then poured himself a nightcap. He went back into the living room and parked himself in the leather La-Z-Boy, set right in front of the 60-inch flat screen television. Using his feet, he pushes off his fifteen-hundred-dollar pair of alligator skin cowboy boots and lets them topple to the floor.

The man was exhausted. As much as he enjoyed – no – *loved* his business trips, they really took it out of him.

The man's name was Peter Ritten. Or "Pistol Pete," as a certain few referred to him.

And his business was murder for hire. And he was the best at it. At least that's the way he felt. He wasn't what he'd call a, "Cheap, dime bag, durag-wearing hitman". Like the oblivious ones you might find on Craigslist if you looked hard enough. And if you were stupid enough.

No, he was an independent contractor for *one* organization.

The same organization that had hired him three times previous this latest job. And the same organization that operated a Raleigh cab company as just one of its many legitimate fronts. The same people, who employed the driver who had dropped Ritten off that night (And three nights previous) with his payment inside of a duffle bag in the trunk.

As with each time before, Ritten hadn't counted the jobs payment yet. There was no need. These people weren't like the gangbangers that resided just a few more miles down Rosewood Ave, that would skim you for a penny if they could. These were professionals, who paid promptly and in full each time. For if no other reason, because they knew they would be in need of his services again. They paid well, too. Fifteen thousand to twenty-five thousand for each job. The stakes had been just a bit higher on this last job, so he'd been thrown an extra five for how clean it had come out.

Clean, of course meaning that no one was caught.

And so Ritten sat in his expensive luxury chair, drinking his expensive scotch, and watching an old western on his expensive television. Laughing as an outlaw Robert Ryan tried kicking a bounty hunting James Stewart off of his horse and down a cliff. Watching this made him think about how smooth things had gone on his last job.

Interpretation: How well he'd managed to blow out the back of a man's head and get away before anyone around had any real idea what had happened.

#5

Gerald Anderson

The Jobs name had been Gerald Anderson. A fifty-two-year-old middle school social studies teacher and father of two that lived in Winston Salem. Mr. Anderson had been unfortunate enough to get his shirts cleaned at a local mob-extorted laundry mat. Of course, he knew nothing about this. For obvious reasons, it wasn't exactly common knowledge that a clandestine criminal organization was bullying a Salem born business man by the name of Ben Goldstein, for "protection" money.

In the midafternoon of October 7th, Mr. Anderson stopped by the mat on his way home from work to pick up his plaid patterned dress shirts from Mr. Goldstein personally. He later recalled how there was no one else inside the shop. Employees included.

Mr. Anderson collected his shirts and paid the bill. Apparently, he and Mr. Goldstein had even engaged in friendly conversation for a minute or two, "Something about the weather I think," Anderson would later say, though he couldn't completely recall that part. And as Anderson was leaving, and they were saying their "Have a good days" and "See you next times," Anderson noticed a man on the sidewalk, heading straight for the mats doors. And being the good Samaritan that he was, Mr. Anderson held the door open for the man. The tall and burly man, who according to Anderson, went out of his way to not look him in the eye and say thank you.

At the time, this didn't bother Anderson in the least. He figured it was just basic everyday rude human behavior, or that maybe the man had been having a bad day. Not thinking twice about it, Mr. Anderson left the mat and made his way over to his Honda Accord parked across the street. Mr. Anderson said, that after carefully placing his freshly pressed shirts in the back of his car like he always did, that he got a call from his wife, Dorothy. She had wanted to know if he'd passed the Harris Teeter on his way back home yet, and when he said no, she asked him if he would stop for hamburger buns and Sprite. After he said that he would, she brought up the topic of how their oldest son, David, might be in need of a math tutor. And after about five minutes of on the phone deliberation, they both agreed to wait on the matter until the latest report cards were sent home. Anderson said that after he hung up and twisted the key to the ignition, that he barley caught the end of a traffic report about an accident that was "slowing things up" on his usual route home.

At that point he glanced back across the street and noticed the big man who had entered the mat just as he was leaving, walking back out. Mr. Anderson said that the man, who he could positively identify because of his height, stocky build, and silver receding hair with thick sideburns, strutted out of the laundry mat, glanced quickly from left to right, and then climbed into the passenger side of a black Cadillac parked in front of the store (that Anderson didn't remember seeing going in) that then pulled away.

And Mr. Anderson, again, not believing that there was anything peculiar about this, did too.

~ ~ ~

The next day, while relaxing in his own La-Z-Boy and drinking a diet coke that he hadn't finished during dinner, Anderson flipped on the evening news. Dan

Forino, or "Dan the man" as Gerald called him, was talking about the latest American casualties in Iraq. Apparently two young Marines were killed when the driver ran over some sort of Improvised Explosive Device.

"Truly tragic..." Dan the man finished. "...And now we take you live to the scene of a grisly murder in Chasm County, with reporter Maria Gonzalez. Maria, what can you tell us about this?"

The screen changed from Dan Forino sitting safely behind his desk, to a young, attractive woman holding a microphone with a big WBC11 stamped on it. The woman was standing in front of a large crowd of people gathered around police cars, all of which had their lights on and flashing. Uniformed police could be seen walking up and down, patrolling the line of yellow tape used to blockade the sidewalk. Mr. Anderson was too busy checking out the reporter, who's shirt could have been buttoned once or twice more and been much less revealing, to notice the building that was now being referred to as a crime scene, was the laundry mat he'd been visiting every other week.

Including yesterday.

"Dan, details are still scarce..." Said the young woman after a second of silence pressing at the device in her ear, presumably to better hear what Dan the man was saying. "...but officials are saying that local business man and owner of the laundry mat located right behind me on Brad street, Benjamin Goldstein, was found inside the mat yesterday, murdered..."

That was enough to get Anderson's attention.

"...Police are telling us that Mr. Goldstein's body was discovered by one of his own employees, who had been out on an early lunch break, apparently by Goldstein's request, and that when he returned he found Benjamin Goldstein unconscious on the floor behind the counter, with what appeared to be some sort of, *wire* around his neck. Now police aren't saying whether they have any suspects, but if you have any information regarding this crime you should immediately dial Crime Stoppers..."

Mr. Anderson did call Crime Stoppers. Almost immediately. He had to rewind the two-minute broadcast a few times to be sure that he wasn't mishearing the dead man's name. But he wasn't. And after he took his eyes off the pretty reporter's chest long enough to look behind her, and through the swarm of on-lookers, he knew it was the laundry mat. And after telling the misses (who was reluctant at the idea of him getting involved) about what he'd seen the day before and what he'd seen that night, he made the call.

Crime Stoppers was more than interested in what Mr. Anderson had seen. So much so, that they redirected him to the man in charge of the case, a Detective William Stauner. Stauner had Anderson meet him at the station that very night. As it turned out, the police *did* have a suspect. His name was Donnie Burke, and he looked the same in his printed-out mugshot as he did the day Anderson saw him.

After he told the Detective that there was no doubt that that was the man he'd seen that day, and that "Yes" he'd be willing to point him out in open court and say so, Mr. Anderson's fate was sealed.

~ ~ ~

That was where Ritten came in.

Weeks later, after it had been made apparent that Mr. Anderson, the sole witness, was the D.A.'s only hope for a conviction against the local gangster, and after the leak inside of the W.S.P.D let the mob know the name and address of the canary who had decided to sing against them, Ritten was given the contract.

He spent the next week tailing Gerald Anderson, observing his everyday movement; memorizing his routine. He'd watch Anderson pulling into the school parking lot each weekday morning, then eight hours later he'd watch him pull back out. He'd watch him Tuesday and Thursday afternoon, when he took his thirteen-year-old and his eleven-year-old to their karate lesson. He'd watch him as he made regular stops to the grocery store to pick up various items his wife had forgotten on her own trip there. And he'd watch him stop at the local Kangaroo Koffee shop every day after work, no matter what. For at least fifteen minutes at a time.

And on a Friday, his last day of observation, that was where Ritten decided he'd kill Mr. Anderson.

~ ~ ~

The following Monday, around 4:30 p.m.

Ritten, disguised as a vagrant, wearing a bushy fake beard and an L.A. Laker's cap, along with a worn Army jacket, made his way across the parking lot of the shopping center where Kangaroo Koffee was located. Stumbling along the way, as to give an intoxicated impression and to make sure he did not reach Mr. Anderson's car before he did.

Anderson had just walked out of the shop, a coffee still in his hands. And being parked so close to the front doors, he was already using his free hand to find the car keys in his Khakis. Ritten carefully made his way around the back of a parked mini-van covered in, "Baby on Board!" decals, parked beside Mr. Anderson's Honda. As the school teacher balanced his coffee cup on the roof of his car and shuffled through his set of keys to find the right one, Pistol Pete Ritten approached him from behind with his hands stuffed into his coat pockets. His right hand was wrapped around a snub nose .38, that after dousing in bleach, he would later dispose of.

He was ready to give Anderson the ol', "Got any spare change, mister?" line. But after he was already pointing the gun at the back of the man's head, he didn't think it mattered anymore. He squeezed the trigger once and the unsuspecting Mr. Anderson's head gave a violent jerk forward, stippling the cars side with blood. Anderson dropped to the ground without rolling over, leaving the newly formed crater exposing the back of his skull for all the world to see.

Ritten fired two more shots into the dead man's back (you know ... just to be sure...) as a group of teenage girls who had previously been glued by the eyes to their smartphones, fled from the picnic tables and into the coffee shop, screaming as loud as they could. The girls fled into the Kangaroo Koffee while Ritten ran back to the other side of the parking lot, through an alley between a nail saloon and a soccer store, and down a dirt hill to the abandoned lot of an old warehouse, where he'd left the stolen Lincoln that had been provided for him, running. He hoped in, threw it in gear, and "put the pedal to the metal," making his way to Mill Street (removing his synthetic facial hair and cap as he did so). A street that would quickly get him to the highway, and away from the bloody, long lasting chaos he had created.

~ ~ ~

It would be more than safe to say that Ritten had enjoyed shooting Anderson. Not because of the money. Don't get it wrong, he loved the money. And he never faced the dreaded dilemma of what to spend it on. But he *wanted* to shoot Anderson. Not Anderson personally, just somebody. Anybody really. The fact that he got paid for it was just what he considered a bonus. He knew that in the normal world he'd be considered sick. Even psychopathic by definition. But that didn't bother him in the slightest. If anything, he was glad he wasn't repressed by societies generic guide of moral ethics.

It meant he could do *whatever* he wanted, to *whoeve*r he wanted.

Why?

Because fuck em' that's why.

Ritten had been like this for as long as he could remember. And the misanthropy that resided inside of him only prospered more and more as each day passed. Why should he care about people? No one ever did anything for him, and he didn't want them to. It was a cold, lonely, dog-eat-dog world, and that was just the way he wanted it. Besides, what he did for a living was only a mouse squeak compared to the racket the government made in the world of malevolence and murder. So, what if he got by doing what they did on a smaller scale? If you like something and you're good at it, you shouldn't do it for free. Right?

Even if you probably would.

~ ~ ~

Ritten was sitting in his chair, rattling the melting ice around in his drink, and philosophically belittling the entire world and its problems while watching the cowboys on TV hide from a thunderstorm inside of a cave. He watched as Robert Ryan's character was challenged to a draw by James Stewart's (the same character he'd failed to murder earlier). The cowboy became noticeably stirred at the likely hood that he'd fail to draw his gun faster than the bounty hunter. Ritten cheered on for the outlaw on his TV to, "Fucking go for it!" When the obviously discomfited Ryan froze on the screen. For a moment, Ritten just thought the man was paralyzed from fear at the prospect of death. But then in some strange sort of glitch, the cowboys face – his fearful eyes and quivering mouth were still moving, but there was only silence. No talking. Not even the sound of rain that should have been pouring and roaring in the background. Only the still, scared cowboy breathing heavy and looking more and more anxious at whatever was supposed to be happening on the other side of the camera.

"Ah, come on!' Ritten shouted in aggravation. "Is this what I'm paying so much for?"

For a minute, Ritten could only see the image of a frozen killer who didn't like having the tables turned on him. Then the sound cut in.

But it wasn't the piece of dialogue that it should have been. Ritten didn't know what it was at first. It sounded sort of familiar, but he couldn't place it and it didn't fit the scenario of the movie he had been watching.

"Clarence! I wanna' live again! I wanna' live again!" Came booming in over the image Ritten had been staring at dubiously. "What the fuck..." he muttered to himself.

"I wanna' live again!"

Then he placed it. Why it sounded so familiar. It was still James Stewart's voice speaking, only it was the wrong movie. Ritten had never seen the entire thing, but he knew that that was the line the actor cathartically proclaimed on a bridge at the end of It's a Wonderful Life.

Jesus, he thought. *Not only is this thing frozen in some bizarre new way of being frozen, but now the end of another movie is playing on top of it.*

"Please God, let me live again." Begged the ghost inside the television.

"Wow," Ritten said, "What the hell else could they fuck up?"

216

Then, ironically enough, the TV went black. The picture of an intimidated outlaw was gone, and the pleas of a repenting man went with it.

Ritten, even more upset now, challenged the TV by pressing the red power button on the controller again and again and again. Nothing happened, the screen only offered darkness. Ritten smacked the remote against the palm of his hand twice before giving up and tossing it to the floor.

"Guess they'd had enough of James Stewart, too." He said to be purposefully flippant. With a single chuckle, he finished off the watered-down scotch in his glass, then got up to fix another. Being careful as to not step on his expensive boots; the same he'd earlier let topple to the floor.

Ritten thought, *whatever. I don't give a shit. I don't need that fake Hollywood action. I've got memories of the real deal rolling around in my head.*

He certainly did.

He got to the bar and scooped out more ice from the bucket, wondering what the girls who had been outside of the shop when he blew Anderson's head off were doing now. And what they said to the cops. "Doesn't matter," He tells himself. The only thing they could say was that they were all busy sexting different boys on their fancy phones when they heard a bang and looked up to see some homeless guy running across the street. "That'll get 'em far," Ritten says, laughing in his head. And then out loud. He picks up the same bottle of Johnnie Walker and starts to pour another drink but stops before the liquor can pass through the neck of the bottle. There's something ... different. The bottle ... It was lighter.

What? No, that doesn't make any sense.

It is. It's lighter. This thing was half full twenty minutes ago, and now there's less than a third left!

So, who snuck in and drank some *of it?*

That's stupid, he thinks filling his glass. *I guess I just poured myself a better drink than I realized. I do feel good.*

Anyway.

Anderson, HA! That had been fun. He'd have done the job even if the guy had been Mahatma Gandhi reincarnated. But the fact that Anderson was what men like Ritten like to call a rat, only made it that much more satisfying. Another notch on his gun, so to speak.

Yes, he'd enjoyed killing Anderson, plenty. But this quick, inane paranoia about missing booze made him think about Tommy Gravette.

His third job. And hell, his favorite.

#3

Thomas Gravette

The murder of Thomas Gravette had been the hit that earned Peter Ritten the moniker, "Pistol Pete," amongst the mobsters who employed him, because of the sheer brutality and cold-blooded nature in which it was carried out.

Ten years prior to the day of his murder, and about eight years before Ritten would go into business, Gravette had been an out of town stick-up man brought into Fayetteville for a five-man bank heist, organized by some of the more "out there" figures in the organization. A bank heist, in which a teller and a security guard were both killed. It was known amongst the men in charge that Gravette had a bit of a drinking problem, but at the time it was widely believed that he had it under control, for the most part. Plus, most of the other men on the job, sent about an 8 ball of coke up their nose every day. So, they didn't reflect on how that might've been an issue for a getaway driver with a nervous temperament.

It was.

~ ~ ~

While four men, armed with shotguns held up the Fairmount Bank, Gravette sat in the driver's seat of the getaway car just outside the banks doors. He was drinking from a pint of cheap Smirnoff (his second that day) that he kept on him, while waiting for his ski-masked comrades to rush out through the doors beside him and hop back into the car.

Right about the time Gravette was getting queasy, and regretting how he'd skipped breakfast that morning, he heard the first blast from what he knew was a shotgun from inside the bank. Then the second. All at once paranoia, fear, and drunken nausea enveloped Gravette. He'd been hired to drive the car for a heist job, not a *murder*. It didn't matter that all he did was drive, he was a part of it. And that was the difference between ten years and the gas chamber. The thought was enough to send the drunken getaway driver on his way before the rest of the passengers had returned. But he didn't get very far.

The intoxicated and frightened Gravette threw the car into drive and without looking, immediately pulled out in front of an SUV that had been passing by at 40 mph. It smashed into the left side of the stolen Impala and sent the undamaged right side of the car into the Subaru that was parked in front of him.

The robbers came running out of the building, only to find their getaway car crumpled up in the street next to some other shit heap. With their drunk wheelman slumped over the front seat.

One witness, who had also seen the car crash and stopped to help, said one of the masked men was so infuriated that after shouting, "Are you fucking kidding me?" that he grabbed him by his lapels and threw him to the curb, before climbing into his Audi with the other men and fleeing the scene.

He said he felt lucky to be alive.

~ ~ ~

Gravette survived his car accident. And lucky for him the only thing broken was his arm. He was lucky because if he had injured his jaw he might not have felt as talkative as he did when the FBI came to visit him in the hospital; with a deal. A deal he took as soon as the word "Immunity" was mentioned. No contemplation needed.

And after not only the other robbers were arrested, but also the men who had orchestrated the caper were as well, it didn't take much debate to figure out who was talking. Or what was going to happen to him. The only problem for the gang, as far as revenge was concerned, was that the deal Gravette had taken included Witness Protection. A new Identity, location, everything. But the mob knew Gravette was a fuck-up. Unfortunately, more so now than ever. And that it was only a matter of time before he screwed up enough for the feds to get tired of it and kick him to the curb.

And almost a decade later, that's exactly what happened. After one too many "small time" drug deals, the then full blown alcoholic Thomas Gravette, was given his final new identity and let go from the WitSec program. It didn't take too long for the bosses on the street to get word that Gravette was living in Atlanta under the name Ronald Murphy.

It seemed like the perfect job for an up and coming gunman they had discovered.

Ritten thought so, too.

~ ~ ~

After a week of being followed, a drunk an unwary man going by the name Ronald Murphy, staggered down a flight of stairs to the second story of a parking garage to find the car that he was much too drunk to legally drive. This had become routine for him, because for the last month he had, for all intents and purposes, been living with a prostitute named "Anastasia," whose apartment he had just come from. He wouldn't have even left if he hadn't been running low on Schnapps. He pushed past the door to the stairway and started across the lot. And then he dropped his car keys for the second time since leaving the apartment.

"Fuck," was the last thing the man said aloud, while bending over strategically, as to retrieve his keys without falling over. Not noticing the man who had been following him for the last week, come out from the shadows provided by the Pepsi machines close by, until he heard the echoing of boot heals, letting him know that he wasn't alone. Pistol Pete raised the revolver in his hand, the same kind of "Burner" he had, and would, always use. And fired once.

The bullet hit the rising man, who had only just realized what was going on, through the left eye. Killing him instantly.

Ritten knew Gravette was dead. But just the same, he went over and stood above the body, and then fired the remaining four shots into the dead man's face; totally disfiguring him. Not because it was a sure and professional way of making sure the job was done, but just because he wanted to.

~ ~ ~

Days later, before a cab with his payment in the trunk would take him home for the second time, Ritten was invited to have a drink with some of the gangsters who were pleased with the way Gravette had been taken care of. An invitation he was happy to accept.

As the liquor flowed, the men laughed and laughed as Ritten gave his detailed account of how Gravette's face had exploded each time he sent another round through it. Finally, one of the older men raised his bourbon and proclaimed, "I've got it! Pete! Pistol Pete!" Several others raised their glasses and nodded their heads in approval.

"Yea!"

"Pistol Pete!"

"Long live Pistol Pete!"

~ ~ ~

Rittens reminiscing of turning a man's face into bloody ground beef began to wrap-up as he ascended the stairs to the second story of his home. Travel suitcase in one hand, duffel bag full of cash in the other. He flipped a switch and there was light in his bedroom. The bed was still neat and made proper, just the way he left it.

Man, that looks good, he thought. His eyes had only gotten heavier since arriving back home, and after rinsing the pomade out of his hair, a good shave, and maybe a third drink, he'd be ready for hibernation. But first, he'd have a look inside the bag. He wouldn't count the money tonight; too tired. He just wanted to look at it. He pulled the zipper open, flung the bag upside down, and let the stacks of money fall to the bed. It always surprised him how little thirty-thousand dollars in cash looked in person, but there it was.

Christ, if it were all in hundreds they wouldn't even need a duffel bag. They could just give it to me in an envelope.

Ritten rubbed his chin as he gawked down to the small mountain of currency laying on top of his bed. He could feel the thin layer of stubble growing from his face. He hadn't shaved since the night before he killed Mr. Anderson. He supposed that it might've been that facial rug he'd had to wear that threw him off his regular grooming cycle. He went into the bathroom connected to his own room, down to only his trousers and wife beater, and splashed some warm water from the sink onto his face. As he dabbed his face with the towel he caught a glimpse of the face looking back at him in the mirror.

His own.

The face of death.

He didn't understand why, but there was something about looking into his own eyes that sent a chill up his spine, making every hair on his body stand at attention as it went. What's that old expression? It was like someone had walked over his grave. But Ritten enjoyed these sudden waves of goosebumps that would stir through him. It excited him, for whatever reason. One of the few times he could feel sincere pleasure. For all the television that Ritten watched, he was an avid reader. And the last thing he had begun to enlighten himself upon was a man named, J. Robert Oppenheimer. One of the men considered "The Father of the A-Bomb." He read that after the first atomic bomb had been tested in the New Mexican desert, and as the ominous mushroom cloud of destruction consumed the sky, that some of those involved, had laughed, some had cried, some did nothing at all. Oppenheimer himself, was reminded of a line from an ancient Hindu scripture. "Now I am death, the destroyer of worlds."

The destroyer of worlds...

I am the destroyer of worlds, Ritten thought. Staring coldly into his own reflection.

I am death.

Rittens moment of morbid introspection passed as he remembered why he had come into the bathroom in the first place. He reached for his barber brush to smear the shaving cream and stopped halfway to laugh when he remembered that he'd left his shaving kit in his travel bag.

"Figures," he said, heading back into the bedroom. *Well could be worse, could have forgotten the mone ...* The smell hit him first. He didn't think much of it the split second before looking up, just that the air had a metallic fragrance. And then he saw it. The penny-like stenches source, cloaked the money on his bed. It was covering all the bills and most of the blue silk sheets below. The combination of red and blue should have created a sort of dirty diluted purple, but there was only red. Blood red. He couldn't be for sure it was blood, just that it sure appeared to be.

And if it looks like blood, and it smells like blood...

Ritten dashed to the nightstand and retrieved the .357 magnum he kept holstered behind it. Someone was here, in his home. Someone had done this to his money, deliberately toying with him. Who it was and why? Well he'd find that out.

After searching every hiding place upstairs, including in the closest and under the bed, a barefoot Ritten raced down the stairs, magnum up and ready. All he could think of was, *who? WHO? And how the fuck did they get in here and do that without me noticing? They couldn't have. Which means they were already in the house, waiting. But how could I not hear them sneaking around in my room, pouring blood all over my fucking bed. I was right in the next room, and with the door open. And for less than a minute!*

Ritten stormed through the first story of the house. Swinging each bathroom and closet door wide open, sticking his revolver into the darkness ahead of him each time. He found nothing. Ritten parked himself in the middle of the room, and in a blind rage flung his La-Z-Boy over on its side. It was all he could do to stop himself from shooting and breaking shit. He stood, wondering, *how? It's impossible, there's nowhere to hide that I haven't checked. Whoever it is, they're still here. I got down here too quick to not hear a door opening or closing. Upstairs, I must have overlooked something upstairs.* Ritten pulled back the hammer to his gun and trotted back up the staircase.

"Alright you fuck, where are..." The sentence fell short when he got back into the room and saw the money.

I'm going mad. Totally out of my mind, bat-shit fucking mad!

The blood that had been caked all over his money was gone, and the pile of cash was now spotless. So why could he still smell it?

Ritten stepped forward, cautiously. Revolver aimed up and ahead, like the bed itself was the root of all the trouble. For all Ritten knew it might be. There wasn't a trace of blood. Not even any of the rubber bands securing the money had red on them. With his finger off the trigger and resting on the guard, Ritten rubbed at his temple with the barrel of the gun.

This just keeps getting crazier and making less and less sense. How are they doing this? They couldn't have cleaned it off that fast. The goddamn money doesn't even look like its moved, and the sheets seem fresher than ever! So why can I still smell that fucking blood?

Ritten got his answer as soon as he turned to look around. On the wall behind him, in big bold print, written in blood, was a message.

YOUR BLOOD MONEY HAS BEEN CLEANED
HA-HA-HA-HA-HA

The first thing that went through Ritten's mind was that this was the stupidest fucking joke he'd ever heard *or* read. But that was quickly subsided by another thought. A memory really. The memory of a woman named Ashlee Shaw. Or better known to Ritten as the fourth job.

#4
Ashlee Shaw

Ashlee Shaw had been a forty-one-year-old mother of three. She had also been a criminal attorney who helped structure the entire money laundering operation for the Durham faction of the mob. And for five, long, profitable years she'd done well by them, helping start up almost a dozen legitimate businesses that were used to camouflage the not so legitimate earnings of the organization (including a cab company that would spread through the state). With only a few of them going under. Dive bars and strip joints mostly, that all seemed to burn to the ground in similar incidents. Incidents that made insurance collecting inevitable. But they couldn't blame her for these. Just as they couldn't blame her for the R.I.C.O. indictment that would come, seizing several of their businesses along with dozens of their members.

But just because they *couldn't* blame her for this, didn't mean they weren't going to.

~ ~ ~

On an early morning in May, a mobster named Bruno Gibbons took a telephone call from a Detective Limely. Detective Richard Limely, a degenerate gambler who'd be lucky if he made it to the age of fifty, owed Gibbons twenty-three thousand dollars in gambling debts. He informed Gibbons that a woman by the name of Ashlee Shaw, had been picked up by FBI agents who had been using the precinct as their base of operation over the last two months, and that they had been pressing her hard for information over the last hour. After telling Gibbons that he didn't know anymore, because neither he or his fellow officers were allowed to use their own interview room while the FBI was using it, Limely hung up. Only to call back four hours later to let Gibbons know that the Shaw woman had been released.

~ ~ ~

Almost approximately twenty-four hours later, when Bruno Gibbons sat handcuffed in the back of 1 of 2 goon-packed vans being driven by FBI agents, it never occurred to him that Ms. Shaw, while in fact being takin to the police station by federal agents and released just five hours later, refused the obvious deal she was offered. And after hours of unsuccessful reasoning, she was let go only to be followed by more agents, who believed that they would catch her in the act of tipping off her Mafioso partners. Which she didn't. Which lead to her not going to jail with the rest of them. Which, in turn, lead to Bruno Gibbons vindictively musing over the message he would soon pass of to his lawyer. It was a concise message.

Shaw woman. Kill her.

~ ~ ~

Two weeks after Ritten was given the contract on Ashlee Shaw he was ready to make his move. He took an extra week of surveillance this time because Shaw was divorced, with three children. Which meant that at any time, there could be at least four other guests in her three-story suburban home. Which was where Ritten planned to kill her. Luckily for Ritten, the ex-husband, who never came around (not even to pick up his own kids, she always dropped them off), followed the draconian child custody agreement to a tee. Which meant that every Friday through Tuesday, the kids were at their father's house and Shaw was alone in hers. On both of the Friday nights Ritten spent tailing Ashlee

Shaw he followed her to the Marriott, where she would meet her friends in the bar (Ritten presumed other lawyers as well, just based on the pants suits the women were wearing) and spend the next few hours drinking martinis and flirting desperately with the younger busboy. This was where Ritten devised his plan.

That next Friday, after Ashlee Shaw hopped in her Beamer and sped off to indulge in her Friday night ritual, Ritten broke into her house through the back door. He used a rock he wrapped in a bandana to smash out a corner of the window, then reached in and unlocked the door. He knew that she kept a spare key underneath the larger of the flower pots out on the front porch. He'd seen her use it plenty of times from his car when her hands were too full to go digging through her purse for her own key. But leaving a messy (yet at the same time, meticulous) break-in scene was part of his plan.

He got to work, knowing that at the most he had maybe four hours before Shaw would return. He unplugged the TV downstairs and lifted it off the wall it was attached to and laid it on the floor. Then he went upstairs into what looked like Shaw's bedroom, unplugged the TV there, and brought it down next to the other. Then, grabbing a garbage bag from under the sink, he went back up into the bedroom to fill it with the jewelry boxes he'd seen on the dresser. He filled the bag with everything on the surface and a few watches he found in the drawers. Then he went to the closest, looking for a safe he might be able to add to the monetary pile of shit he was creating downstairs in this woman's living room. He didn't find a safe, but he found something else. Something that brought a crooked smile to his face and a maniacal laugh to go along with it. Behind the array of colorfully organized woman's shoes, and poorly shielded by a UNC college sweatshirt was a shotgun. Ritten picked it up and was delighted to see the elegant floral engraving along the barrel and stock of the gun. He couldn't begin to imagine that it might've been hers, or at least that it was she who bought it. It wasn't just some cheap 20 gauge anyone could have purchased at Wal-Mart a few years ago. It was a sportsman's over and under shotgun; the kind rich, pipe smoking gentlemen in expensive plaid sports jackets with patches on the elbow used to shoot clay pigeons while they drank bourbon and talked about the stock market. Ritten hit the switch on top of it and was even more shocked to see that there was a shell in each barrel. He didn't think upper middle class suburban folk kept their guns loaded. Maybe she just didn't know about it, Ritten didn't see a box of shells while he was pillaging through the draws. Then again, thinking of the current relationship she had with the men who'd sent him here, maybe it *was* loaded on purpose.

Of course, he had his traditional "throw away" .38 in his coat pocket. But using the woman's own gun would only make the scenario Ritten was trying to create even more plausible. He'd stacked enough of her valuables on top of each other to make it look like he was heisting the place. Which was exactly what he wanted. And now he was hiding in the linen closest by the vestibule with Ashlee Shaw's shotgun, waiting, and wanting for her to come home so he could carry out the finale of his 'wrong place, wrong time' staging.

As time passed, he began to worry that the first thing she might see when she came into the den was all of her junk that he'd left there, and that she would just turn around and run. But after about an hour and a half of waiting in the dark he heard a car door slamming outside and knew that it was too late to do anything about it. But once again, luck was on Ritten's side, because as he peered through the shades of the closet, the woman he saw come through the front door was too busy yapping on the phone to notice anything immediately strange. Ritten could tell she was drunk; every other word that came out of her mouth was slurred. He could see that she wasn't even five feet from the door yet and hadn't flipped on the lights.

"Why should I have to pay more?" she spoke bitterly on the other side. "You're his father, you should pay for half his car, not less than a third of it!"

There was a moment of silence, presumably so the dickhead ex-husband could spew about why he didn't have to pay as much as she should.

"Because he's turning sixteen, that's why!" She finally said. Even through his narrow, darkened view, Ritten could see the scowl form on Shaw's face as she said, "Oh ... Oh fuck you, Tom!"

She ended the call with the argumentative Tom and then hurled the phone across the room onto the couch. That was when she noticed all her costly house hold accessories stacked up in her living room. The words "what the hell?" slipped silently past her lips as a tall stranger emerged from the closet, holding a very familiar looking weapon. There was a frighteningly pleased grin on the man's face as he raised the shotgun in her direction. Ashlee Shaw wanted to shout, *NO!* She wanted to say *Please don't!* She wanted to plead for her life to this disturbingly excited gunman aiming her own shotgun at her, with a smile on his face that was clear even in the shadows of the room. Most of all she wanted to scream. She wanted to scream louder and longer than any of those damsels in distress from the old horror movies. She wanted to scream because she knew that even if there was time to beg this man not to kill her, not even for her sake, but for her three children's, that it would make no difference. The fiendishly evil look in the stranger's eyes made that clear.

There was a quick, brilliant flash accompanied by an explosion. And there was only darkness and silence for Ashlee Shaw.

~ ~ ~

The police statement issued to the press regarding the murder of Ashlee Shaw Attorney at law, couldn't have been narrated any better if Ritten himself had written it. There was no mention at all of her alleged mob ties. Only witness statements from her girlfriends who all said that the last time they saw her was at the bar for routine girl's night drinks, and that she left for home somewhere between 10:30 and 11:00 pm, just like she always did. The media went on to say, that based on evidence gathered in the deceased's home, that police speculated that Ms. Shaw had walked in on an active burglary taking place in her home, and that the man or men involved had murdered her with an expensive shotgun her ex-husband had left her in the divorce, that they must have found while rummaging through the house. Police said the murder weapon was located at the scene, with no trace of the intruder(s) left behind.

The case is active and ongoing.

If you have any knowledge of this crime or those involved, please dial Crime Sto...

~ ~ ~

The Shaw woman, Ritten thought. *Someone's comeback to get me for that Shaw bitch. Who the hell would care about her? I never saw a boyfriend or even a neighbor with a crush hanging around. The ex-husband, Tom, maybe? Doubtful. I didn't tail him or even look into his background, so for all I know the guy could be a fucking navy seal. But the way they were going at each other on the phone, I think it's more likely that I did him a favor rather than an injustice. Christ, that guy's probably just happy that he doesn't have to pay alimony anymore. Then WHO?*

All these thoughts and possibilities raced around the track of Ritten's mind as he was once again trudging downstairs. Revolver still up and ready.

"Ok, alright I get it. You're here because of that Shaw bitch, right?" Ritten asked the empty room. "Well, what're you gonna' do about it?"

Nothing.

"I said what the hell are you gonna' do about it?" Ritten repeated, louder, spinning in place next to his overturned chair, eyeing every nook and cranny of the down stairs.

The room didn't respond.

Ritten began to giggle. "You can't just be here to write on my wall with, what? Cows blood?" The giggle turned into a laugh, and then it became hysterical. Then all at once he was done laughing.

"Got some bad news for ya though, Mr. Punisher. I think when I'm done here, I'm gonna' head over to Durham with a can of gas and burn down whatever house those ugly little rug rats of hers sleep in now. Maybe you wanna live long enough to come watch that with me?"

Once again, the room didn't respond to Ritten.

What kind of avenger is this guy? Is he planning on just hiding in the walls (or wherever the fuck he is) until I go to sleep? Is he gonna' stay hidden if I say, "See ya, I'm off to Durham for a bonfire!" And Jesus, who the hell is he?

All kinds of questions and possibilities crossed Ritten's mind, until he noticed something rather insignificant, considering his current situation. His expensive boots, the same ones he'd shimmed off with his feet and let topple to the floor from the reclined position of his La-Z-Boy, were now upright. Side by side. And not even close to the foot rest anymore. *But I just let them drop to the floor. They couldn't have landed so perfectly, I'm sure of it. And the shine on them... I always keep em' clean, but Jesus, it looks like someone just got done buffing them.*

Why? Why, would somebody sneak into his house – not to kill him – but to draw on his wall like a child and to shine his shoes like it was their fucking job.

This new, confounding element in an already confusing and unsolved puzzle only infuriated the flummoxed Ritten. It wasn't that someone had messed with his possessions or vandalized his wall. It wasn't even that someone had broken into his home. It was that somebody was playing with him. Playing with him, like a cruel child plays with ants and a magnifying glass. And soon enough, they would try and burn him.

"Where are you?" Ritten asked – no – demanded. "Come out now, Goddamnit! No more of this hide n seek shit!" He was screaming his orders now. "I wanna know who's here, I wanna see you!"

Before he had time to realize what he was doing or to stop himself, Ritten fired a shot into the ceiling. And after he did, he was still too furious to hate himself for it.

"*Now!* Show yourself, *now!* Come on! Come on, what're you waitin' for, huh? I'm right fuckin' here. Where are you?"

"We're here. With you, Ritten." The room finally answered back.

Ritten had no reason to recognize the voice coming from behind him, but he did. He knew who was there.

"Do you remember us Ritten?"

Peter Ritten's head slowly crept over his shoulder as he turned around, his eyelids creeping open as he did so.

"...Oh my God..."

#1 and #2

George Fitzgerald and Sally Pierson

The first human being that Peter Ritten killed professionally was an 18-year-old kid named George Fitzgerald. At the time of his death, George had been out of high school for almost a year and still wasn't sure what his calling in life was supposed to be. When he was even younger, ten maybe, George's grandfather would tell him war stories (the less gruesome ones) from his time in Vietnam, and for years after his grandfather's death he dreamed of joining the army.

But as a freshman in high school – right about the time he noticed girls wanting to get closer to him, rather than as far away as they could for fear of cooties – he thought he wanted to be an actor, such as so many other young men his age. Late at nights, when he was supposed to be getting his brain sleep for the school day to come, he would spend hours looking at the formidable reflection he created in his mirror and repeated the infamous Deniro line, "Are *you* talkin' to *me*?"

This ambition rattled around in his head for the next couple of years. Until one day, just about the end of his junior year, a neighborhood friend convinced him to go into the Deli shop down the street from their apartment complex. That might not have been such a life altering decision if it had been any old deli shop they went into, but it wasn't. Hell, George only agreed to go because he was sick of the McDonald's that they visited every other day, which was the only other place to eat within walking distance. There were only so many ingredients you could add to a mcdouble to make it taste like something other than a mcdouble. Anyway, the deli had a certain, *rapport,* in that part of town. George used to hear his parents joking about how it was like the cab stand filled with gangsters at the beginning of that movie Goodfellas. And how they didn't want their son to end up hanging around those people, like the young man in the movie did.

But that's what wound up happening the day he ventured into the deli. At least, for the next two years.

~ ~ ~

Call it fate if you want, but that day in the shop while the two boys waited for their sandwiches to be brought to their table, Georges friend chose that moment – for no particularly obvious reason – to give George a little history lesson on his girlfriend at the time. A history lesson, in which she had apparently slept with at least *two* guys on *each* of the sports teams that their school had to offer. And after ignoring the request made by George for him to keep his mouth shut, the friend went on with the next bit of locker room gossip. This time about his girlfriend and the gym couch. That was when George threw the first blow. Only he didn't hit him with his fist, he hit him with the metal napkin dispenser on the table next to the salt and pepper, bashing his friends nose in a direction it wasn't meant to go. The friend tumbled backwards in his chair and onto the floor. Both of his hands were cupping his nose, trying desperately to stop the blood gushing from his face. George shot from his chair, throwing the table out of his way so swiftly it was like he didn't even know it was there. He brought the small metallic box down onto the boy's face for a second time, breaking two of the fingers covering his mouth and chipping a tooth beneath them.

And as he raised the box to deliver a third strike, George felt the hand of a giant wrapping around his wrist.

"Christ, kid..." The voice of the giant said. "...You're about to beat your lil' buddy to death in my shop. I gotta hard enough time with the health inspectors and cops, as it is."

The bloody appliance George had used as a weapon slid from his grip as he turned to see who the hand grasping his wrist belonged to. What he saw was a man who had to be at least six feet five, with dark oily hair, in an expensive looking suit. The smell of cigars lingered around him, even though George saw none.

Ah Jesus, George thought. *This one of the guy's moms always talking about. I really stepped in it this time.*

"Al, take that kid out the back and take him to a fuckin' hospital." The Giant told the grey-haired man in the apron who'd been behind the counter making subs the whole time. "Tell 'em he got mugged by some crackhead around the corner. And make sure that's the way *he* remembers it too."

As the man named Al escorted a bloody and sobbing teenager through the hallway and out the back, the giant finally released George's hand from his possession. Sizing him up as George rubbed his aching wrist.

"What'd you do that for, kid?" The man asked.

"He pissed me off."

George's response made the giant laugh, but he didn't say it so matter-of-factly because he was a taciturn tough guy. He said it because he was nervous, and it was the shortest, most concise version of the truth.

"I missed the start of the show 'cause I was back in my office, but I caught the end there." The giant said, pointing thick fingers that were bearing large, golden rings at the overturned table and small blood specs smeared on the floor, just inches away. "You would've kept hittin' him if I hadn't stopped you, wouldn't you've?"

George thought so, but he didn't say it.

The giant smiled. "I like you, kid. You got somethin' that's gettin' harder and harder to find in people these days. What's your name?" Asked the gangster who would have George murdered almost two years later.

~ ~ ~

Over the next two years, George spent most of his afternoons in the Deli shop. Mostly shining men's shoes and playing watchman at the front door when they told him to. And every once in a while, they'd give him a box or an envelope to deliver around the neighborhood. Mostly to other businesses where the employees looked and talked just like the men in the deli. He made a weekly salary of two hundred dollars, but he'd pull twice that in tips. It was unbelievable. He'd shine one man's shoes and get a twenty, then another's and he'd get a fifty! He loved getting paid three times as much as normal kids his age, to mostly clean a pair of shoes and listen to wise guys sit around and shoot the shit. After the first month, he'd had a change of heart regarding his career choice, and quickly forgot that he'd ever wanted to help spread democracy to foreign lands or play a lonely, embittered cab driver.

~ ~ ~

Then one day, right around the second year of his employment, George went into work and found the place empty. A lot of times during the work day, especially before George came in, the guys would hang out in the back, drinking fine liquor and telling racist jokes. But Al was always up front behind the counter. Always, no matter what. Except that day.

"Al?"

When no one answered George, he had the fatal idea that maybe they were in the room at the end of the hallway. The room they were always in on those days he'd been told to stand out front and tell people the shop was closed. He'd never been in there before, but he'd never been told *not* to go in there either.

Well, George thought, *couldn't hurt.*

He was wrong and found that out quickly.

~ ~ ~

The first thing George saw when he opened the door to that room he'd never been in before, was Al and another man that everybody called "John Boy" rolling a man into a dirty old rug spread on the floor. The man was dead, that was obvious. His face, bloody and swollen, looked like it had been stung by every bee in the hive. Al let go of the dead man's feet and John Boy stopped trying to roll the rug over him. Both of their eyes were as wide as deer about to be demolished by an 18-wheeler.

"Jesus kid, you scared the shit outta me!" John Boy had apparently said. "I thought you were ... well ... what the hell are you doin' back here?"

George didn't answer. They said all his attention was on the corpse in the rug.

"Look Georgie, don't come back here no more, unless we tell you to. Got it?"

George nodded, without looking away from it.

Later, John Boy would tell the others how he felt nervous about how the kid was staring at the man in the rug. He said that all the stories he'd heard about Georgie almost beating someone to death with a restaurant accessory like it was nothing contradicted what he saw in the kid's eyes that day.

Utter terror.

John Boy said he gave the kid a hundred-dollar bill and the rest of the day off. Told him to go get ice cream or whatever kids do.

~ ~ ~

When John Boy and Al first told the rest of the gang about what the kid had seen, none of them were too worried about it. George had been spending a lot of time with them over the last couple of years. He'd listened to their crazy stories while he shined their shoes, and delivered dozens of packages for them, that he had to have known weren't exactly, "On the level." None of them thought it was too big a deal that he'd seen the body in the shop. Everyone assumed that he was being groomed into one of them anyway, and that this was going to happen sooner or later. They thought that after two or three days of bad dreams and a queasy stomach, that he'd be back, ready to work and joke about it. But after the first week of George not showing up for work, they became concerned. Half way through the second, they became suspicious. And at the beginning of the third, they decided that George had to die. It would've been different if he'd quit without seeing a dead man in their shop being prepared for disposal, but he had. George knew too much to not be one of them anymore. Besides, there was another newcomer they wanted to give a chance. And this one was eager to pull the trigger.

~ ~ ~

Ritten murdered George and his girlfriend, Sally Pierson, nearly two weeks later by the river underneath a city bridge. An isolated spot where teenagers could spend their afternoons indulging in the sweaty fantasies that consumes so many young people's leisure time. Ritten had followed George and his girlfriend to the towns lover's lane, and decided to do it there, quickly. He parked by the bridge and strutted down the walkway and saw George's Jeep Wrangler parked close to the water. His strut turned into a halfhearted jog, and when he reached the driver's side he flung the door open. George, who had apparently not noticed Ritten coming towards them, never knew what hit him. There was a quick flash and then nothing. Ritten reassured that with a second shot to the head. George's lifeless body slumped over onto the lap of the pretty young blonde in a sunflower dress screaming her head off. She was just at the wrong place at the wrong time, at least that's what Ritten would say. But he knew she was in the car, he just didn't give a shit and that's all there really was to it.

Sally spent the last five seconds of her life crying and begging her dead boyfriend to *"Wake up! Please, wake up!"* as she wiped the blood from Georges face off her own. And then Ritten fired the last three shots into her chest. Silencing her for what he thought would be forever. After taking the dead couples purse and wallet – to make it look like a robbery – Ritten took off as fast as he could. He felt a little anxious carrying their belongings, but they'd be gone soon enough. Along with the cheap, duct tape handled .38 he'd gotten from the same giant gangster who had once smiled at George and told him he liked him.

Oh well, Ritten thought. *Worth the risk. I'm sure I'll get a few grand more for the trouble of that dead blonde bitch. Or at the very least another job offer.*

Yea, another job. That's what I want. That's what I really want.

~ ~ ~

Back in the respectable neighborhood of Five Points, Peter Ritten's Elderly neighbor, Mrs. Bradshaw, wakes in her bed to the sound of a single thunderous bang. She had fallen asleep watching Yankee Doodle Dandy, and when she saw that James Cagney was still dancing on her TV screen, she knew she hadn't dozed off for very long. She put on her night robe and stepped into her slippers, then pulled back the blinds of her window. Everything was quiet and dark on Maple street.

Except for Mr. Ritten's house next door. There were several lights on in that house. All of them, maybe.

Mrs. Bradshaw had only met Peter Ritten a few times since he'd moved into the neighborhood, mostly passing hellos, and he didn't exactly seem, amiable. But she thought maybe he could be hurt. She knew perfectly well that the bang that had awakened her was a gunshot. She'd heard plenty of them back on the ranch with her husband, before cancer had taken him from her, and sent her into the city to escape the painful memories. She put her dentures in and spun the telephone dial for the police.

"911, what's your emergency?" Came the woman's voice on the other end of the line.

"Hello? Yes, this is Mrs. Elma Bradshaw of 5668 Maple street, and well... I do hope it's nothing, but I'm quite sure that I just heard a gunshot coming from next door at the home of a nic... of a young man named Mr. Ritten. All of his lights seem to be on, and that shot sounded terribly close."

"Yes ma'am, we've already received several calls about a gunshot coming from that street and a unit is on its way there now."

242

"Other calls? Really? Oh, I do hope It's nothing serious."

"A patrol car will be there shortly ma'am. In the meantime, remain in your home with the doors locked.

"Yes. Yes, thank you. Goodnight."

Mrs. Bradshaw laid the phone on the receiver and went back to the window, waiting to see a police car that would pull up at any moment.

"I hope it's nothing serious." She said again, this time to herself.

I'd hate to think Mr. Rittens in trouble.

~ ~ ~

"Do you remember us, Ritten?" George Fitzgerald asked. He was wearing the same dress shirt and jeans he'd been wearing that day in the Jeep. And there were still bullet holes in his head. One crude gash that almost merged with his eye, and another just above his temple.

Sally, the young blonde in the sunflower dress who had been at the wrong place at the wrong time, stood beside him. Her breasts that should have been covered by summer warm yellow flowers, were instead stained with blood. Fabric ripped in the spots where the bullets had torn into her.

Despite all of that, neither of them would have looked alive anyway, the sickly pallid skin and vacant glare said it all.

"...Oh my God..."

"I knew that you would," said the ghostly figure of the boy Ritten had murdered.

"No ... You're dead. Both of you ... dead..." The last word came out sounding more like a question.

"Still very observant, aren't you, Mr. Ritten?" This time a woman spoke, but it wasn't the bloody blonde that stood in front of him. Ritten turned his head and saw that Ashlee Shaw was standing next to him. The

Grand Canyon of shotgun wounds he'd left in her stomach, still very much there.

"You…"

"Yes, Mr. Ritten. Its me."

Ritten shook his head like a child who refused to take the bad news. "I killed you … I fucking killed you!"

"Yea you did Ritten. Just like you killed me."

Ritten turned and saw the monstrosity behind him.

"I'm a little harder to recognize, ain't I? Well, that's because of you."

Ritten had no problem recognizing Thomas Gravette, even though he looked … different. Much, different. The face of the man, that had been ripped apart by Ritten's cruel doings – along with the assistance of five metal capsules, looked as though it had been crudely pieced back together with a skin colored glue stick. Its nose was slanted, one eye was now inches higher than the other, and his mouth that hung ajar (he didn't seem to be able to close it) exposed the teeth that now had gaps, inches wide between one another. He looked frightfully similar to Leatherface from Chainsaw Massacre. Except that wasn't a skin-mask he was wearing, that was *his face*.

"Oough, what the fffuck…" Ritten said, his top lip curled in a repulsed scowl.

"Ugly right? Yea, thanks for that. Lucky for me, looks don't really matter where I am now."

Where I am now?

"Where … where you are … now?"

Gravette laughed. Or Ritten thought he did, really it sounded more like a cackling smokers cough. "Don't worry, Ritten. You'll find out all about that."

Jesus, Ritten thought. *I'm in the fucking Twilight Zone.*

"What about him?" Gravette asked raising his finger. "Do you remember him? Surely if you remember us, you remember him."

Ritten's head kept spinning until he reached the final piece of the haunted circle surrounding him. And there, right in front of him, was Gerald Anderson. The same man Ritten had gunned down in a parking lot in front of a group of teenagers. And he was sure, that if he took a look behind Anderson, the gory crater he'd put into the back of his head would still be there.

"Hello, Mr. Ritten."

Another one of his victims voices he was hearing for the first time.

Things were starting to ... Well ... not make sense ... but come together. The shined shoes from the kid, the missing booze from Frankenstein's monster (formally known as Gravette), and the blood money (literally) being cleaned by the Shaw bitch. He didn't know a thing about Sally (including her name), so for all he knew she could've done his dishes or stolen his cd's. And hell, he bet that if he'd had any of his old school work lying around, that Anderson would've gone through and regraded it all. Real fucking scary.

Ritten began to laugh. Loudly.

"Ok. *OK*, I get it." He said, "So, you've come back from the dead, for revenge..." He was still laughing. "...and your idea of that is to, what, drink my booze and spit shine my boots?" His laughter was hysterical now. "Well I gotta tell ya, that's pretty fuckin' *spooky!*"

"We only wanted you to remember, Ritten," said Shaw's ghost, dripping blood from the hole in her stomach onto the carpet. "But you don't have any trouble remembering us, do you, Ritten?"

He didn't answer. But he did stop laughing.

"And revenge," now it was Anderson who spoke; his head moving slowly from left to right, his dead eyes never blinking. "That is not what this is."

"Yea? Well before I wake up from this crazy, prolonged nightmare, why don't one of you tell me what *this* is?"

A second passed. And then another.

And then each ghastly pale figure took a simultaneous step toward Ritten. Enclosing the circle they'd formed around him.

"*We're here to tell you what you've done.*" The bitter voice of George was speaking again. Or at least it was his voice that could be heard, his lips had stopped moving. "*You and your murderous bosses had every right to be worried! I was indeed planning on going to the police about what I saw that day in the shop, and dozens of lives would have been saved if I'd been able to!*"

"I don't have any *bosses*! No one tells me what to do!" Ritten said. Only it sounded more like he was telling it to himself.

"*No Mr. Ritten, you don't have any bosses. You just know people who are dumb enough to pay for what you like to do.*" It was Sally's voice this time, frustrated and surprisingly deep. "*When my father got the news of how his only daughter had been killed, he dropped dead on the front door. His heart just gave out when they told him!*"

Ritten didn't speak, he just spun in place, looking into the face of each of the figures closing in on him. His revolver raised waist level.

"*And I, Ritten!*" Gravette's voice. "*I would have killed a family of three, not to mention myself, in a drunken highway accident. But you didn't empty your gun into my face because of that. You did it because you enjoyed it!*"

"*Back!*" Ritten hissed. "Back goddamnit!" His gun was now up past his torso.

"*What about me, Ritten? Do you care what I would have done with my life?*" Anderson asked. The ghostly voices being spoken through closed lips only grew louder as the circle around Ritten grew smaller.

"*Or what happened to my loved ones?*" Shaw.

"*Do you care at all?*" Sally.

"*No. No, you don't. DO you?*" George.

"Shut up! Shut up! Shut up! *SHUT THE FUCK UP!*" Ritten screamed as the compilation of pained voices began to speak all at once, on top of each other.

"*What about me?*"

"*And me?*"

"*Yes, what about it Ritten?*"

All at once. And it was starting to sound like more than just the five voices of the slowly moving beings, who were now almost close enough to reach out and touch Ritten. It seemed like the voice of every soul who had ever been wronged by another were all coming down and questioning Ritten.

"*Why?*"

"*Why?*"

"*You're evil!*"

"*What about me?*"

The words were all getting louder; louder and piling up more and more on top of each other. No breaks between the countless sounds of sorrow. Ritten shut his eyes as tight as he could, so tight that it hurt. He threw his hands over his ears, the cannon against his head. "*Ahh, God stop! Stop! Stop it! Make it fucking stop!*"

"*Ritten!*"

"*Ritten.*"

"*Why me, Ritten?*"

He could feel how close they were when a chill passed through his body, filling him with goosebumps that he wasn't enjoying.

"*WHY?*"

"**WHY?**"

"AH JUST SHUT UP!" He opened his eyes, and Gerald Anderson was standing inches in front of him, smiling. They were all smiling. Ritten aimed the long barrel right down between Anderson's eyes and fired.

Anderson vanished. That was all, nothing else. Like he was never there.

Ritten spun left and put his sights on the gaped tooth smiling Gravette and fired.

Gravette vanished.

He spun to Ashlee Shaw and fired. And Shaw was gone.

Then to George and Sally, who were still standing close to one another. Ritten shot, first into Sally and then into George, and they were gone with the others, but the voices didn't stop. They were louder now, screaming really.

"*Ritten!*"

"*Ritten!*"

"*You're a monster, Ritten!*"

Ritten dropped to his knees, and gave a deep, final yell with his chin up, then gritted his teeth, shut his eyes, and stuck the barrel of the gun against his temple.

"*Do it!*"

"*Do it now!*" the voices commanded.

The cylinder spun and the hammer dropped. And the voices stopped all together. But Ritten was still alive. His revolver was out of bullets.

And then there was laughter. A woman's laugh. Old and raspy, like a cackling witch.

Then it was joined by a man's laugh. Then another. Another woman's, next.

As Ritten opened his eyes, though all the figures were gone, the voices were back. And they were laughing at him. All of them.

Louder. And louder, and *louder*.

Ritten shot to his feet and took off down the hall for the front door, hands back over his ears, still holding the gun.

The laughter amplified as he fled. It was *inside* of his head now. Echoing.

"Stop it! Stop! Just shut up!" Ritten bellowed as he flung the front door open and dashed out into the night.

~ ~ ~

Meanwhile .... As Peter Ritten shoots at ghosts in his living room, a patrol car carrying Sergeant Robinson and Sergeant Bishop turns off Arkin Rd and onto Maple street. As Robinson drives, Bishop takes the radio and holds down the button when it's by his lips.

"This is car 18, we can already hear shots coming from Maple, send additional units."

"Roger car 18"

"That lady said she thought it was coming from 5667 Maple, right?"

"Roger that."

"Alright, we're on the scene."

"Roger car 18, additional units are in route."

"You see that?" asked Robinson, pointing with a hand on top of the steering wheel. Bishop leaned forward and looked up. There was a man and a woman, peering out through their curtains in the house across from 5667. Their shadows profiled by what looked like a television flashing behind them. Next door was the same. An older man, who hadn't bothered putting on a shirt, was at his own window looking out. Those who weren't looking at the police car seemed to be watching 5667. The house with all its lights on.

"Yea, I see it. That means no one will be too tired to answer questions."

Robinson parked at the curb, a few feet from where a city cab had parked earlier that night.

"Alright, get your gun out," said Bishop. "This neighborhood isn't exactly the Gardens down Rosewood, but those were defiantly gunshots we heard."

"Right," said Robinson, taking off his seatbelt and unsheathing his recently purchased and approved for the line of duty Glock .40.

The officers got out and ambled carefully down the sidewalk, realizing that everyone with a decent windows view on Maple street was watching them. They stopped just before 5667's walkway began.

"Alright Robinson, Listen. I want you to go arou..."

That was when they heard shouting. Someone telling someone else to "Shut up" and to "Stop it." And then a man came flying out the front door of 5667. A tall man, wearing only his pants and undershirt. He was holding a gun. The man jumped off the porch, completely ignoring the stairs. Stumbling as he landed on his bare feet, almost tripping completely over but managing to keep trucking forward. He only stopped when he saw the two cops on the sidewalk pointing their guns at him and demanding that he, "Drop the fucking gun!"

"They're inside!" the man shouted, pointing his sizable revolver back towards the house. "They came back! They're inside, there!"

"Sir, drop it now! Drop the gun!" one cop yelled.

"Drop the fucking gun right now man, do it!" yelled the other.

"I said they're back! They came ba..." When the man waved the gun away from the house, the officers must have decided that he'd done that one too many times after being warned, and one of them opened fire. The other joined, and bullets buried themselves into Ritten's chest. He stumbled backwards as bits of shirt and skin exploded, and Pistol Pete Ritten was dead before he hit the ground.

The cops stopped shooting. They watched as the supine man's bent knee stilled, then flopped down by the other. Then the man was completely still.

Robinson and Bishop looked to one another, each wandering what the neighbors watching them would say when asked about this later.

~ ~ ~

Maple street was flooded with blue strobing lights and crowds of people, neighbors and on lookers alike, all trying to get a peek and see what all the fuss was about. Yellow Do Not Cross tape kept everyone at bay, except for the police and forensics unit on the scene. A shape under a white blanket is loaded into the back of an ambulance. Beside the bus, a burly man with a grown-out buzz cut and a two-day beard, who has already unbuttoned his shirt collar and loosened his tie, steps out of a blue Crown Vic. He finishes what looks like a coffee, and then hands the cup off to one of the many uniforms around him. He walks around the crowd and ducks under the yellow barrier, showing his badge to the cop on guard duty, and makes his way to the porch, where a short, bespectacled man in a suit is waiting. The man looks up, sees him coming and says, "Hey there, Johnson. Long night?"

"Fuck you, Bill." He replies. "What do we got here?"

"Single white male, late twenties, Peter Ritten. Our boys Robinson and Bishop responded to a shots fired report, and said when they got here this fella Ritten came running out of the house waving his gun around, which, turned out to be empty except for the spent-shell casings inside, blabbing about someone inside of his house. The next responding unit arrived and searched the place. There was nothing. Only thing they found that seemed peculiar was in the upstairs bedroom. Pile of cash, not sure of the amount yet."

"Cash, huh?" Johnson said, following the short man into the house. "Nothing else in the room?"

"Nothing."

They went into the living room and stood almost exactly where Ritten had last been. The short man in glasses named Bill points first to the ceiling, and says, "So, he fires there, there, there, there, there, and there. Then runs outside for whatever reason, runs into our boys out there, waves the gun around, they don't know its empty, and he gets himself shot. Neighbors stories collaborate."

Johnson pulls his tie even looser as he examines the room. He asks, "Said someone was in here, huh?"

"That's right. Our guys said they couldn't catch everything he was spitting out, but that part was perfectly clear. I'm sure the lab results will show that the guy was higher than Dennis Hopper in the 70's."

"Maybe." Johnson said without looking away from the tv he was now standing in front of.

Bill studies him for a moment, then asks, "Anything good on?"

Johnson finally looks back at him, "You notice anything?"

Bill stuffs both hands in his pockets and takes a quick glance around the room before answering, "He liked westerns?"

"You're a real Columbo, ain't you?"

Bill smiles. "Alright, then what?"

Johnson aims his finger at the shattered TV screen. "Well, let's just assume, for the sake of investigating, that the tv was off when he shot it."

Bill shrugs. "Ok."

"Now, along with the blank TV screen he put a bullet in, he also shot that tiny mirror beside you, hooked up on the bar."

Bill turns to his left and observes the shards of glass on the floor.

"Now, he also shot that big framed movie poster that you noticed on the wall behind you."

Bill turns to look at the big-framed poster of The Wild Bunch. Half of the poster is solid black with the casts' names at the bottom, Bill can just see the bullet hole in the middle of his foreheads reflection. He adjusts his glasses, turns back to Johnson and again, shrugs. "Ok."

Johnson goes on. "Then over here, he shoots through both of the windows to these twin cabinets."

Bill sighs, "So what, Johnson? What's your point?"

Now Johnson stood exactly where Ritten had when confronted by the ghosts of his past.

"The blank TV screen, the mirror, the poster frame, the two cabinet windows that are side by side. My point is, besides that lonely round up there in the ceiling ... everything this guy shot was some form of reflective glass."

Bill looks right into Johnson's eyes, squinting, and turning his head like he could find another angle that would somehow make his friend's train of thought easier to follow. Then he takes one more look around, at each piece of evidence surrounding them, and finally says, "And what? He didn't like the mug looking back at him?"

Bill laughed.

Johnson didn't. "Yea. Yea, maybe."

"Jesus, Johnson you really need some sleep."

"Shut up, Bill. Come on let's finish up here and I'll buy you a coffee," Johnson said, stepping over Ritten's sprawled boots.

===

About the Author

A young writer from Raleigh, NC, Nick Swain's publication history includes several works of crime fiction featured in Crimson Streets Magazine; this includes the Neo-Noir heist story "The LaFierra Caper and Its Rat Pack Robbers"; the one-room gangster mystery "The Cabanga Situation"; and the serialized novella "Devil in Disguise"; along with an engaging guide for aspiring Pulp writers and avid readers alike titled "Fast Talk: The Slang of Pulp."

Swain has also had an eerie tale published in each of HellBound Books' "Shopping List" anthologies. "The House on the Back Road" being featured in the first, and "Archie's Beachside Paradise" being featured in its sequel.

NewPulpPress.com

www.ingramcontent.com/pod-product-compliance
Lightning Source LLC
Chambersburg PA
CBHW060539260626
47161CB00003B/977